Petty Troubles of
Married Life

Honoré de Balzac

PREFACE

IN WHICH EVERY ONE WILL FIND
HIS OWN IMPRESSIONS OF MARRIAGE.

A friend, in speaking to you of a young woman, says: "Good family, well bred, pretty, and three hundred thousand in her own right." You have expressed a desire to meet this charming creature.

Usually, chance interviews are premeditated. And you speak with this object, who has now become very timid.

YOU.—"A delightful evening!"

SHE.—"Oh! yes, sir."

You are allowed to become the suitor of this young person.

THE MOTHER-IN-LAW (to the intended groom).—"You can't imagine how susceptible the dear girl is of attachment."

Meanwhile there is a delicate pecuniary question to be discussed by the two families.

YOUR FATHER (to the mother-in-law).—"My property is valued at five hundred thousand francs, my dear madame!"

YOUR FUTURE MOTHER-IN-LAW.—"And our house, my dear sir, is on a corner lot."

A contract follows, drawn up by two hideous notaries, a small one, and a big one.

Then the two families judge it necessary to convoy you to the civil magistrate's and to the church, before conducting the bride to her chamber.

Then what? . . . . . Why, then come a crowd of petty unforeseen troubles, like the following:

PART FIRST

THE UNKINDEST CUT OF ALL.

Is it a petty or a profound trouble? I knew not; it is profound for your sons-in-law or daughters-in-law, but exceedingly petty for you.

"Petty! You must be joking; why, a child costs terribly dear!" exclaims a ten-times-too-happy husband, at the baptism of his eleventh, called the little last newcomer,—a phrase with which women beguile their families.

"What trouble is this?" you ask me. Well! this is, like many petty troubles of married life, a blessing for some one.

You have, four months since, married off your daughter, whom we will call by the sweet name of CAROLINE, and whom we will make the type of all wives. Caroline is, like all other young ladies, very charming, and you have found for her a husband who is either a lawyer, a captain, an engineer, a judge, or perhaps a young viscount. But he is more likely to be what sensible families must seek,—the ideal of their desires—the only son of a rich landed proprietor. (See the *Preface*.)

This phoenix we will call ADOLPHE, whatever may be his position in the world, his age, and the color of his hair.

The lawyer, the captain, the engineer, the judge, in short, the son-in-law, Adolphe, and his family, have seen in Miss Caroline:

I.—Miss Caroline;

II.—The only daughter of your wife and you.

Here, as in the Chamber of Deputies, we are compelled to call for a division of the house:

1.—As to your wife.

Your wife is to inherit the property of a maternal uncle, a gouty old fellow whom she humors, nurses, caresses, and muffles up; to say

1

nothing of her father's fortune. Caroline has always adored her uncle, —her uncle who trotted her on his knee, her uncle who—her uncle whom—her uncle, in short,—whose property is estimated at two hundred thousand.

Further, your wife is well preserved, though her age has been the subject of mature reflection on the part of your son-in-law's grandparents and other ancestors. After many skirmishes between the mothers-in-law, they have at last confided to each other the little secrets peculiar to women of ripe years.

"How is it with you, my dear madame?"

"I, thank heaven, have passed the period; and you?"

"I really hope I have, too!" says your wife.

"You can marry Caroline," says Adolphe's mother to your future son-in-law; "Caroline will be the sole heiress of her mother, of her uncle, and her grandfather."

2.—As to yourself.

You are also the heir of your maternal grandfather, a good old man whose possessions will surely fall to you, for he has grown imbecile, and is therefore incapable of making a will.

You are an amiable man, but you have been very dissipated in your youth. Besides, you are fifty-nine years old, and your head is bald, resembling a bare knee in the middle of a gray wig.

III.—A dowry of three hundred thousand.

IV.—Caroline's only sister, a little dunce of twelve, a sickly child, who bids fair to fill an early grave.

V.—Your own fortune, father-in-law (in certain kinds of society they say *papa father-in-law*) yielding an income of twenty thousand, and which will soon be increased by an inheritance.

VI.—Your wife's fortune, which will be increased by two inheritances —from her uncle and her grandfather. In all, thus:

Three inheritances and interest,	750,000
Your fortune,	250,000
Your wife's fortune,	250,000
Total,	1,250,000

which surely cannot take wing!

Such is the autopsy of all those brilliant marriages that conduct their processions of dancers and eaters, in white gloves, flowering at the button-hole, with bouquets of orange flowers, furbelows, veils, coaches and coach-drivers, from the magistrate's to the church, from the church to the banquet, from the banquet to the dance, from the dance to the nuptial chamber, to the music of the orchestra and the accompaniment of the immemorial pleasantries uttered by relics of dandies, for are there not, here and there in society, relics of dandies, as there are relics of English horses? To be sure, and such is the osteology of the most amorous intent.

The majority of the relatives have had a word to say about this marriage.

Those on the side of the bridegroom:

"Adolphe has made a good thing of it."

Those on the side of the bride:

"Caroline has made a splendid match. Adolphe is an only son, and will have an income of sixty thousand, *some day or other!*"

Some time afterwards, the happy judge, the happy engineer, the happy captain, the happy lawyer, the happy only son of a rich landed proprietor, in short Adolphe, comes to dine with you, accompanied by his family.

Your daughter Caroline is exceedingly proud of the somewhat rounded form of her waist. All women display an innocent artfulness, the first time they find themselves facing motherhood. Like a soldier who makes a brilliant toilet for his first battle, they love to play the pale, the suffering; they rise in a certain manner, and walk with the prettiest affectation. While yet flowers, they bear a fruit; they enjoy their maternity by anticipation. All those little ways are exceedingly charming—the first time.

Your wife, now the mother-in-law of Adolphe, subjects herself to the pressure of tight corsets. When her daughter laughs, she weeps; when Caroline wishes her happiness public, she tries to conceal hers. After dinner, the discerning eye of the co-mother-in-law divines the work of darkness.

Your wife also is an expectant mother! The news spreads like lightning, and your oldest college friend says to you laughingly: "Ah! so you are trying to increase the population again!"

You have some hope in a consultation that is to take place to-morrow. You, kind-hearted man that you are, you turn red, you hope it is merely the dropsy; but the doctors confirm the arrival of a *little last one*!

In such circumstances some timorous husbands go to the country or make a journey to Italy. In short, a strange confusion reigns in your household; both you and your wife are in a false position.

"Why, you old rogue, you, you ought to be ashamed of yourself!" says a friend to you on the Boulevard.

"Well! do as much if you can," is your angry retort.

"It's as bad as being robbed on the highway!" says your son-in-law's family. "Robbed on the highway" is a flattering expression for the mother-in-law.

The family hopes that the child which divides the expected fortune in three parts, will be, like all old men's children, scrofulous, feeble, an abortion. Will it be likely to live? The family awaits the delivery of your wife with an anxiety like that which agitated the house of Orleans during the confinement of the Duchess de Berri: a second son would secure the throne to the younger branch without the onerous conditions of July; Henry V would easily seize the crown. From that moment the house of Orleans was obliged to play double or quits: the event gave them the game.

The mother and the daughter are put to bed nine days apart.

Caroline's first child is a pale, cadaverous little girl that will not live.

Her mother's last child is a splendid boy, weighing twelve pounds, with two teeth and luxuriant hair.

For sixteen years you have desired a son. This conjugal annoyance is the only one that makes you beside yourself with joy. For your rejuvenated wife has attained what must be called the *Indian Summer* of women; she nurses, she has a full breast of milk! Her complexion is fresh, her color is pure pink and white. In her forty-second year, she affects the young woman, buys little baby stockings, walks about followed by a nurse, embroiders caps and tries on the cunningest headdresses. Alexandrine has resolved to instruct her daughter by her example; she is delightful and happy. And yet this is a trouble, a petty one for you, a serious one for your son-in-law. This annoyance is of the two sexes, it is common to you and your wife. In short, in this instance, your paternity renders you all the more proud from the fact that it is incontestable, my dear sir!

REVELATIONS.

Generally speaking, a young woman does not exhibit her true character till she has been married two or three years. She hides her faults, without intending it, in the midst of her first joys, of her first parties of pleasure. She goes into society to dance, she visits her relatives to show you off, she journeys on with an escort of love's first wiles; she is gradually transformed from girlhood to womanhood. Then she becomes mother and nurse, and in this situation, full of charming pangs, that leaves neither a word nor a moment for observation, such are its multiplied cares, it is impossible to judge of a woman. You require, then, three or four years of intimate life before you discover an exceedingly melancholy fact, one that gives you cause for constant terror.

Your wife, the young lady in whom the first pleasures of life and love supplied the place of grace and wit, so arch, so animated, so vivacious, whose least movements spoke with delicious eloquence, has cast off, slowly, one by one, her natural artifices. At last you perceive the truth! You try to disbelieve it, you think yourself deceived; but no: Caroline lacks intellect, she is dull, she can neither joke nor reason, sometimes she has little tact. You are frightened. You find yourself forever obliged to lead this darling through the thorny paths, where you must perforce leave your self-esteem in tatters.

You have already been annoyed several times by replies that, in society, were politely received: people have held their tongues instead of smiling; but you were certain that after your departure the women looked at each other and said: "Did you hear Madame Adolphe?"

"Your little woman, she is—"

"A regular cabbage-head."

"How could he, who is certainly a man of sense, choose—?"

"He should educate, teach his wife, or make her hold her tongue."

AXIOMS.

Axiom.—In our system of civilization a man is entirely responsible for his wife.

Axiom.—The husband does not mould the wife.

Caroline has one day obstinately maintained, at the house of Madame de Fischtaminel, a very distinguished lady, that her little last one resembled neither its father nor its mother, but looked like a certain friend of the family. She perhaps enlightens Monsieur de Fischtaminel, and overthrows the labors of three years, by tearing down the scaffolding of Madame de Fischtaminel's assertions, who, after this visit, will treat you will coolness, suspecting, as she does, that you have been making indiscreet remarks to your wife.

On another occasion, Caroline, after having conversed with a writer about his works, counsels the poet, who is already a prolific author, to try to write something likely to live. Sometimes she complains of the slow attendance at the tables of people who have but one servant and have put themselves to great trouble to receive her. Sometimes she speaks ill of widows who marry again, before Madame Deschars who has married a third time, and on this occasion, an ex-notary, Nicolas-Jean-Jerome-Nepomucene-Ange-Marie-Victor-Joseph Deschars, a friend of your father's.

In short, you are no longer yourself when you are in society with your wife. Like a man who is riding a skittish horse and glares straight between the beast's two ears, you are absorbed by the attention with which you listen to your Caroline.

In order to compensate herself for the silence to which young ladies are condemned, Caroline talks; or rather babbles. She wants to make a sensation, and she does make a sensation; nothing stops her. She addresses the most eminent men, the most celebrated women. She introduces herself, and puts you on the rack. Going into society is going to the stake.

She begins to think you are cross-grained, moody. The fact is, you are watching her, that's all! In short, you keep her within a small circle of friends, for she has already embroiled you with people on whom your interests depended.

How many times have you recoiled from the necessity of a remonstrance, in the morning, on awakening, when you had put her in a good humor for listening! A woman rarely listens. How many times have you recoiled from the burthen of your imperious obligations!

The conclusion of your ministerial communication can be no other than: "You have no sense." You foresee the effect of your first lesson. Caroline will say to herself: "Ah I have no sense! Haven't I though?"

No woman ever takes this in good part. Both of you must draw the sword and throw away the scabbard. Six weeks after, Caroline may prove to you that she has quite sense enough to *minotaurize* you without your perceiving it.

Frightened at such a prospect, you make use of all the eloquent phrases to gild this pill. In short, you find the means of flattering Caroline's various self-loves, for:

Axiom.—A married woman has several self-loves.

You say that you are her best friend, the only one well situated to enlighten her; the more careful you are, the more watchful and puzzled she is. At this moment she has plenty of sense.

You ask your dear Caroline, whose waist you clasp, how she, who is so brilliant when alone with you, who retorts so charmingly (you remind her of sallies that she has never made, which you put in her mouth, and, which she smilingly accepts), how she can say this, that, and the other, in society. She is, doubtless, like many ladies, timid in company.

"I know," you say, "many very distinguished men who are just the same."

You cite the case of some who are admirable tea-party oracles, but who cannot utter half a dozen sentences in the tribune. Caroline should keep watch over herself; you vaunt silence as the surest method of being witty. In society, a good listener is highly prized.

You have broken the ice, though you have not even scratched its glossy surface: you have placed your hand upon the croup of the most ferocious and savage, the most wakeful and clear-sighted, the most restless, the swiftest, the most jealous, the most ardent and violent, the simplest and most elegant, the most unreasonable, the most watchful chimera of the moral world—THE VANITY OF A WOMAN!

Caroline clasps you in her arms with a saintly embrace, thanks you for your advice, and loves you the more for it; she wishes to be beholden to you for everything, even for her intellect; she may be a dunce, but, what is better than saying fine things, she knows how to do them! But she desires also to be your pride! It is not a question of taste in dress, of elegance and beauty; she wishes to make you proud of her intelligence. You are the luckiest of men in having successfully managed to escape from this first dangerous pass in conjugal life.

"We are going this evening to Madame Deschars', where they never know what to do to amuse themselves; they play all sorts of forfeit games on account of a troop of young women and girls there; you shall see!" she says.

You are so happy at this turn of affairs, that you hum airs and carelessly chew bits of straw and thread, while still in your shirt and drawers. You are like a hare frisking on a flowering dew-perfumed meadow. You leave off your morning gown till the last extremity, when breakfast is on the table. During the day, if you meet a friend and he happens to speak of women, you defend them; you consider women charming, delicious, there is something divine about them.

How often are our opinions dictated to us by the unknown events of our life!

You take your wife to Madame Deschars'. Madame Deschars is a mother and is exceedingly devout. You never see any newspapers at her house: she keeps watch over her daughters by three different husbands, and keeps them all the more closely from the fact that she herself has, it is said, some little things to reproach herself with during the career of her two former lords. At her house, no one dares risk a jest. Everything there is white and pink and perfumed with sanctity, as at the houses of widows who are approaching the confines of their third youth. It seems as if every day were Sunday there.

You, a young husband, join the juvenile society of young women and girls, misses and young people, in the chamber of Madame Deschars. The serious people, politicians, whist-players, and tea-drinkers, are in the parlor.

In Madame Deschars' room they are playing a game which consists in hitting upon words with several meanings, to fit the answers that each player is to make to the following questions:

How do you like it?

What do you do with it?

Where do you put it?

Your turn comes to guess the word, you go into the parlor, take part in a discussion, and return at the call of a smiling young lady. They have selected a word that may be applied to the most enigmatical replies. Everybody knows that, in order to puzzle the strongest heads, the best way is to choose a very ordinary word, and to invent phrases that will send the parlor Oedipus a thousand leagues from each of his previous thoughts.

This game is a poor substitute for lansquenet or dice, but it is not very expensive.

The word MAL has been made the Sphinx of this particular occasion. Every one has determined to put you off the scent. The word, among other acceptations, has that of *mal* [evil], a substantive that signifies, in aesthetics, the opposite of good; of *mal* [pain, disease, complaint], a substantive that enters into a thousand pathological expressions; then *malle* [a mail-bag], and finally *malle* [a trunk], that box of various forms, covered with all kinds of skin, made of every sort of leather, with handles, that journeys rapidly, for it serves to carry travelling effects in, as a man of Delille's school would say.

For you, a man of some sharpness, the Sphinx displays his wiles; he spreads his wings and folds them up again; he shows you his lion's paws, his woman's neck, his horse's loins, and his intellectual head; he shakes his sacred fillets, he strikes an attitude and runs away, he comes and goes, and sweeps the place with his terrible equine tail; he shows his shining claws, and draws them in; he smiles, frisks, and murmurs. He puts on the looks of a joyous child and those of a matron; he is, above all, there to make fun of you.

You ask the group collectively, "How do you like it?"

"I like it for love's sake," says one.

"I like it regular," says another.

"I like it with a long mane."

"I like it with a spring lock."

"I like it unmasked."

"I like it on horseback."

"I like it as coming from God," says Madame Deschars.

"How do you like it?" you say to your wife.

"I like it legitimate."

This response of your wife is not understood, and sends you a journey into the constellated fields of the infinite, where the mind, dazzled by the multitude of creations, finds it impossible to make a choice.

"Where do you put it?"

"In a carriage."

"In a garret."

"In a steamboat."

"In the closet."

"On a cart."

"In prison."

"In the ears."

"In a shop."

Your wife says to you last of all: "In bed."

You were on the point of guessing it, but you know no word that fits this answer, Madame Deschars not being likely to have allowed anything improper.

"What do you do with it?"

"I make it my sole happiness," says your wife, after the answers of all the rest, who have sent you spinning through a whole world of linguistic suppositions.

This response strikes everybody, and you especially; so you persist in seeking the meaning of it. You think of the bottle of hot water that your wife has put to her feet when it is cold,—of the warming pan, above all! Now of her night-cap,—of her handkerchief,—of her curling paper,—of the hem of her chemise,—of her embroidery,—of her flannel jacket,—of your bandanna,—of the pillow.

In short, as the greatest pleasure of the respondents is to see their Oedipus mystified, as each word guessed by you throws them into fits of laughter, superior men, perceiving no word that will fit all the explanations, will sooner give it up than make three unsuccessful attempts. According to the law of this innocent game you are condemned to return to the parlor after leaving a forfeit; but you are so exceedingly puzzled by your wife's answers, that you ask what the word was.

"Mal," exclaims a young miss.

You comprehend everything but your wife's replies: she has not played the game. Neither Madame Deschars, nor any one of the young women understand. She has cheated. You revolt, there is an insurrection among the girls and young women. They seek and are puzzled. You want an explanation, and every one participates in your desire.

"In what sense did you understand the word, my dear?" you say to Caroline.

"Why, male!" [male.]

Madame Deschars bites her lips and manifests the greatest displeasure; the young women blush and drop their eyes; the little girls open theirs, nudge each other and prick up their ears. Your feet are glued to the carpet, and you have so much salt in your throat that you believe in a repetition of the event which delivered Lot from his wife.

You see an infernal life before you; society is out of the question.

To remain at home with this triumphant stupidity is equivalent to condemnation to the state's prison.

Axiom.—Moral tortures exceed physical sufferings by all the difference which exists between the soul and the body.

THE ATTENTIONS OF A WIFE.

Among the keenest pleasures of bachelor life, every man reckons the independence of his getting up. The fancies of the morning compensate for the glooms of evening. A bachelor turns over and over in his bed: he is free to gape loud enough to justify apprehensions of murder, and to scream at a pitch authorizing the suspicion of joys untold. He can forget his oaths of the day before, let the fire burn upon the hearth and the candle sink to its socket,—in short, go to sleep again in spite of pressing work. He can curse the expectant boots which stand holding their black mouths open at him and pricking up their ears. He can pretend not to see the steel hooks which glitter in a sunbeam which has stolen through the curtains, can disregard the sonorous summons of the obstinate clock, can bury himself in a soft place, saying: "Yes, I was in a hurry, yesterday, but am so no longer to-day. Yesterday was a dotard. To-day is a sage: between them stands the night which brings wisdom, the night which gives light. I ought to go, I ought to do it, I promised I would—I am weak, I know. But how can I resist the downy creases of my bed? My feet feel flaccid, I think I must be sick, I am too happy just here. I long to see the ethereal horizon of my dreams again, those women without claws, those winged beings and their obliging ways. In short, I have found the grain of salt to put upon the tail of that bird that was always flying away: the coquette's feet are caught in the line. I have her now—"

Your servant, meantime, reads your newspaper, half-opens your letters, and leaves you to yourself. And you go to sleep again, lulled by the rumbling of the morning wagons. Those terrible, vexatious, quivering teams, laden with meat, those trucks with big tin teats bursting with milk, though they make a clatter most infernal and even crush the paving stones, seem to you to glide over cotton, and vaguely remind you of the orchestra of Napoleon Musard. Though your house trembles in all its timbers and shakes upon its keel, you think yourself a sailor cradled by a zephyr.

You alone have the right to bring these joys to an end by throwing away your night-cap as you twist up your napkin after dinner, and by sitting up in bed. Then you take yourself to task with such reproaches as these: "Ah, mercy on me, I must get up!" "Early to bed and early to rise, makes a man healthy—!" "Get up, lazy bones!"

All this time you remain perfectly tranquil. You look round your chamber, you collect your wits together. Finally, you emerge from the bed, spontaneously! Courageously! of your own accord! You go to the fireplace, you consult the most obliging of timepieces, you utter hopeful sentences thus couched: "Whatshisname is a lazy creature, I guess I shall find him in. I'll run. I'll catch him if he's gone. He's sure to wait for me. There is a quarter of an hour's grace in all appointments, even between debtor and creditor."

You put on your boots with fury, you dress yourself as if you were afraid of being caught half-dressed, you have the delight of being in a hurry, you call your buttons into action, you finally go out like a conqueror, whistling, brandishing your cane, pricking up your ears and breaking into a canter.

After all, you say to yourself, you are responsible to no one, you are your own master!

But you, poor married man, you were stupid enough to say to your wife, "To-morrow, my dear" (sometimes she knows it two days beforehand), "I have got to get up early." Unfortunate Adolphe, you have especially proved the importance of this appointment: "It's to— and to—and above all to—in short to—"

Two hours before dawn, Caroline wakes you up gently and says to you softly: "Adolphy dear, Adolphy love!"

"What's the matter? Fire?"

"No, go to sleep again, I've made a mistake; but the hour hand was on it, any way! It's only four, you can sleep two hours more."

Is not telling a man, "You've only got two hours to sleep," the same thing, on a small scale, as saying to a criminal, "It's five in the morning, the ceremony will be performed at half-past seven"? Such sleep is troubled by an idea dressed in grey and furnished with wings, which comes and flaps, like a bat, upon the windows of your brain.

A woman in a case like this is as exact as a devil coming to claim a soul he has purchased. When the clock strikes five, your wife's voice, too well known, alas! resounds in your ear; she accompanies the stroke, and says with an atrocious calmness, "Adolphe, it's five o'clock, get up, dear."

"Ye-e-e-s, ah-h-h-h!"

"Adolphe, you'll be late for your business, you said so yourself."

"Ah-h-h-h, ye-e-e-e-s." You turn over in despair.

"Come, come, love. I got everything ready last night; now you must, my dear; do you want to miss him? There, up, I say; it's broad daylight."

Caroline throws off the blankets and gets up: she wants to show you that *she* can rise without making a fuss. She opens the blinds, she lets in the sun, the morning air, the noise of the street, and then comes back.

"Why, Adolphe, you *must* get up! Who ever would have supposed you had no energy! But it's just like you men! I am only a poor, weak woman, but when I say a thing, I do it."

You get up grumbling, execrating the sacrament of marriage. There is not the slightest merit in your heroism; it wasn't you, but your wife, that got up. Caroline gets you everything you want with provoking promptitude; she foresees everything, she gives you a muffler in winter, a blue-striped cambric shirt in summer, she treats you like a child; you are still asleep, she dresses you and has all the trouble. She finally thrusts you out of doors. Without her nothing would go straight! She calls you back to give you a paper, a pocketbook, you had forgotten. You don't think of anything, she thinks of everything!

You return five hours afterwards to breakfast, between eleven and noon. The chambermaid is at the door, or on the stairs, or on the landing, talking with somebody's valet: she runs in on hearing or seeing you. Your servant is laying the cloth in a most leisurely style, stopping to look out of the window or to lounge, and coming and going like a person who knows he has plenty of time. You ask for your wife, supposing that she is up and dressed.

"Madame is still in bed," says the maid.

You find your wife languid, lazy, tired and asleep. She had been awake all night to wake you in the morning, so she went to bed again, and is quite hungry now.

You are the cause of all these disarrangements. If breakfast is not ready, she says it's because you went out. If she is not dressed, and if everything is in disorder, it's all your fault. For everything which goes awry she has this answer: "Well, you would get up so early!" "He would get up so early!" is the universal reason. She makes you go to bed early, because you got up early. She can do nothing all day, because you would get up so unusually early.

Eighteen months afterwards, she still maintains, "Without me, you would never get up!" To her friends she says, "My husband get up! If it weren't for me, he never *would* get up!"

To this a man whose hair is beginning to whiten, replies, "A graceful compliment to you, madame!" This slightly indelicate comment puts an end to her boasts.

This petty trouble, repeated several times, teaches you to live alone in the bosom of your family, not to tell all you know, and to have no confidant but yourself: and it often seems to you a question whether the inconveniences of the married state do not exceed its advantages.

SMALL VEXATIONS.

You have made a transition from the frolicsome allegretto of the bachelor to the heavy andante of the father of a family.

Instead of that fine English steed prancing and snorting between the polished shafts of a tilbury as light as your own heart, and moving his glistening croup under the quadruple network of the reins and ribbons that you so skillfully manage with what grace and elegance the Champs Elysees can bear witness—you drive a good solid Norman horse with a steady, family gait.

You have learned what paternal patience is, and you let no opportunity slip of proving it. Your countenance, therefore, is serious.

By your side is a domestic, evidently for two purposes like the carriage. The vehicle is four-wheeled and hung upon English springs: it is corpulent and resembles a Rouen scow: it has glass windows, and an infinity of economical arrangements. It is a barouche in fine weather, and a brougham when it rains. It is apparently light, but, when six persons are in it, it is heavy and tires out your only horse.

On the back seat, spread out like flowers, is your young wife in full bloom, with her mother, a big marshmallow with a great many leaves. These two flowers of the female species twitteringly talk of you, though the noise of the wheels and your attention to the horse, joined to your fatherly caution, prevent you from hearing what they say.

On the front seat, there is a nice tidy nurse holding a little girl in her lap: by her side is a boy in a red plaited shirt, who is continually leaning out of the carriage and climbing upon the cushions, and who has a thousand times drawn down upon himself those declarations of every mother, which he knows to be threats and nothing else: "Be a good boy, Adolphe, or else—" "I declare I'll never bring you again, so there!"

His mamma is secretly tired to death of this noisy little boy: he has provoked her twenty times, and twenty times the face of the little girl asleep has calmed her.

"I am his mother," she says to herself. And so she finally manages to keep her little Adolphe quiet.

You have put your triumphant idea of taking your family to ride into execution. You left your home in the morning, all the opposite neighbors having come to their windows, envying you the privilege which your means give you of going to the country and coming back again without undergoing the miseries of a public conveyance. So you have dragged your unfortunate Norman horse through Paris to Vincennes, from Vincennes to Saint Maur, from Saint Maur to Charenton, from Charenton opposite some island or other which struck your wife and mother-in-law as being prettier than all the landscapes through which you had driven them.

"Let's go to Maison's!" somebody exclaims.

So you go to Maison's, near Alfort. You come home by the left bank of the Seine, in the midst of a cloud of very black Olympian dust. The horse drags your family wearily along. But alas! your pride has fled, and you look without emotion upon his sunken flanks, and upon two bones which stick out on each side of his belly. His coat is roughened by the sweat which has repeatedly come out and dried upon him, and which, no less than the dust, has made him gummy, sticky and shaggy. The horse looks like a wrathy porcupine: you are afraid he will be foundered, and you caress him with the whip-lash in a melancholy way that he perfectly understands, for he moves his head about like an omnibus horse, tired of his deplorable existence.

You think a good deal of this horse; your consider him an excellent one and he cost you twelve hundred francs. When a man has the honor of being the father of a family, he thinks as much of twelve hundred francs as you think of this horse. You see at once the frightful amount of your extra expenses, in case Coco should have to lie by. For two days you will have to take hackney coaches to go to your business. You wife will pout if she can't go out: but she will go out, and take a carriage. The horse will cause the purchase of numerous extras, which you will find in your coachman's bill, — your only coachman, a model coachman, whom you watch as you do a model anybody.

To these thoughts you give expression in the gentle movement of the whip as it falls upon the animal's ribs, up to his knees in the black dust which lines the road in front of La Verrerie.

At this moment, little Adolphe, who doesn't know what to do in this rolling box, has sadly twisted himself up into a corner, and his grandmother anxiously asks him, "What is the matter?"

"I'm hungry," says the child.

"He's hungry," says the mother to her daughter.

"And why shouldn't he be hungry? It is half-past five, we are not at the barrier, and we started at two!"

"Your husband might have treated us to dinner in the country."

"He'd rather make his horse go a couple of leagues further, and get back to the house."

"The cook might have had the day to herself. But Adolphe is right, after all: it's cheaper to dine at home," adds the mother-in-law.

"Adolphe," exclaims your wife, stimulated by the word "cheaper," "we go so slow that I shall be seasick, and you keep driving right in this nasty dust. What are you thinking of? My gown and hat will be ruined!"

"Would you rather ruin the horse?" you ask, with the air of a man who can't be answered.

"Oh, no matter for your horse; just think of your son who is dying of hunger: he hasn't tasted a thing for seven hours. Whip up your old horse! One would really think you cared more for your nag than for your child!"

You dare not give your horse a single crack with the whip, for he might still have vigor enough left to break into a gallop and run away.

"No, Adolphe tries to vex me, he's going slower," says the young wife to her mother. "My dear, go as slow as you like. But I know you'll say I am extravagant when you see me buying another hat."

Upon this you utter a series of remarks which are lost in the racket made by the wheels.

"What's the use of replying with reasons that haven't got an ounce of common-sense?" cries Caroline.

You talk, turning your face to the carriage and then turning back to the horse, to avoid an accident.

"That's right, run against somebody and tip us over, do, you'll be rid of us. Adolphe, your son is dying of hunger. See how pale he is!"

"But Caroline," puts in the mother-in-law, "he's doing the best he can."

Nothing annoys you so much as to have your mother-in-law take your part. She is a hypocrite and is delighted to see you quarreling with her daughter. Gently and with infinite precaution she throws oil on the fire.

When you arrive at the barrier, your wife is mute. She says not a word, she sits with her arms crossed, and will not look at you. You have neither soul, heart, nor sentiment. No one but you could have invented such a party of pleasure. If you are unfortunate enough to remind Caroline that it was she who insisted on the excursion, that morning, for her children's sake, and in behalf of her milk—she nurses the baby—you will be overwhelmed by an avalanche of frigid and stinging reproaches.

You bear it all so as "not to turn the milk of a nursing mother, for whose sake you must overlook some little things," so your atrocious mother-in-law whispers in your ear.

All the furies of Orestes are rankling in your heart.

In reply to the sacramental words pronounced by the officer of the customs, "Have you anything to declare?" your wife says, "I declare a great deal of ill-humor and dust."

She laughs, the officer laughs, and you feel a desire to tip your family into the Seine.

Unluckily for you, you suddenly remember the joyous and perverse young woman who wore a pink bonnet and who made merry in your tilbury six years before, as you passed this spot on your way to the chop-house on the river's bank. What a reminiscence! Was Madame Schontz anxious about babies, about her bonnet, the lace of which was torn to pieces in the bushes? No, she had no care for anything whatever, not even for her dignity, for she shocked the rustic police of Vincennes by the somewhat daring freedom of her style of dancing.

You return home, you have frantically hurried your Norman horse, and have neither prevented an indisposition of the animal, nor an indisposition of your wife.

That evening, Caroline has very little milk. If the baby cries and if your head is split in consequence, it is all your fault, as you preferred the health of your horse to that of your son who was dying of hunger, and of your daughter whose supper has disappeared in a discussion in which your wife was right, *as she always is*.

"Well, well," she says, "men are not mothers!"

As you leave the chamber, you hear your mother-in-law consoling her daughter by these terrible words: "Come, be calm, Caroline: that's the way with them all: they are a selfish lot: your father was just like that!"

THE ULTIMATUM.

It is eight o'clock; you make your appearance in the bedroom of your wife. There is a brilliant light. The chambermaid and the cook hover lightly about. The furniture is covered with dresses and flowers tried on and laid aside.

The hair-dresser is there, an artist par excellence, a sovereign authority, at once nobody and everything. You hear the other domestics going and coming: orders are given and recalled, errands are well or ill performed. The disorder is at its height. This chamber is a studio from whence to issue a parlor Venus.

Your wife desires to be the fairest at the ball which you are to attend. Is it still for your sake, or only for herself, or is it for somebody else? Serious questions these.

The idea does not even occur to you.

You are squeezed, hampered, harnessed in your ball accoutrement: you count your steps as you walk, you look around, you observe, you contemplate talking business on neutral ground with a stock-broker, a notary or a banker, to whom you would not like to give an advantage over you by calling at their house.

A singular fact which all have probably observed, but the causes of which can hardly be determined, is the peculiar repugnance which men dressed and ready to go to a party have for discussions or to answer questions. At the moment of starting, there are few husbands who are not taciturn and profoundly absorbed in reflections which vary with their characters. Those who reply give curt and peremptory answers.

But women, at this time, are exceedingly aggravating. They consult you, they ask your advice upon the best way of concealing the stem of a rose, of giving a graceful fall to a bunch of briar, or a happy turn to a scarf. As a neat English expression has it, "they fish for compliments," and sometimes for better than compliments.

A boy just out of school would discern the motive concealed behind the willows of these pretexts: but your wife is so well known to you, and you have so often playfully joked upon her moral and physical perfections, that you are harsh enough to give your opinion briefly and conscientiously: you thus force Caroline to put that decisive question, so cruel to women, even those who have been married twenty years:

"So I don't suit you then?"

Drawn upon the true ground by this inquiry, you bestow upon her such little compliments as you can spare and which are, as it were, the small change, the sous, the liards of your purse.

"The best gown you ever wore!" "I never saw you so well dressed." "Blue, pink, yellow, cherry [take your pick], becomes you charmingly." "Your head-dress is quite original." "As you go in, every one will admire you." "You will not only be the prettiest, but the best dressed." "They'll all be mad not to have your taste." "Beauty is a natural gift: taste is like intelligence, a thing that we may be proud of."

"Do you think so? Are you in earnest, Adolphe?"

Your wife is coquetting with you. She chooses this moment to force from you your pretended opinion of one and another of her friends, and to insinuate the price of the articles of her dress you so much admire. Nothing is too dear to please you. She sends the cook out of the room.

"Let's go," you say.

She sends the chambermaid out after having dismissed the hair-dresser, and begins to turn round and round before her glass, showing off to you her most glorious beauties.

"Let's go," you say.

"You are in a hurry," she returns.

And she goes on exhibiting herself with all her little airs, setting herself off like a fine peach magnificently exhibited in a fruiterer's window. But since you have dined rather heartily, you kiss her upon the forehead merely, not feeling able to countersign your opinions. Caroline becomes serious.

The carriage waits. All the household looks at Caroline as she goes out: she is the masterpiece to which all have contributed, and everybody admires the common work.

Your wife departs highly satisfied with herself, but a good deal displeased with you. She proceeds loftily to the ball, just as a picture, caressed by the painter and minutely retouched in the studio, is sent to the annual exhibition in the vast bazaar of the Louvre. Your wife, alas! sees fifty women handsomer than herself: they have invented dresses of the most extravagant price, and more or less original: and that which happens at the Louvre to the masterpiece, happens to the object of feminine labor: your wife's dress seems pale by the side of another very much like it, but the livelier color of which crushes it. Caroline is nobody, and is hardly noticed. When there are sixty handsome women in a room, the sentiment of beauty is lost, beauty is no longer appreciated. Your wife becomes a very ordinary affair. The petty stratagem of her smile, made perfect by practice, has no meaning in the midst of countenances of noble expression, of self-possessed women of lofty presence. She is completely put down, and no one asks her to dance. She tries to force an expression of pretended satisfaction, but, as she is not satisfied, she hears people say, "Madame Adolphe is looking very ill to-night." Women hypocritically ask her if she is indisposed and "Why don't you dance?" They have a whole catalogue of malicious remarks veneered with sympathy and electroplated with charity, enough to damn a saint, to make a monkey serious, and to give the devil the shudders.

You, who are innocently playing cards or walking backwards and forwards, and so have not seen one of the thousand pin-pricks with which your wife's self-love has been tattooed, you come and ask her in a whisper, "What is the matter?"

"Order *my* carriage!"

This *my* is the consummation of marriage. For two years she has said "*my husband's* carriage," "*the* carriage," "*our* carriage," and now she says "*my* carriage."

You are in the midst of a game, you say, somebody wants his revenge, or you must get your money back.

Here, Adolphe, we allow that you have sufficient strength of mind to say yes, to disappear, and *not* to order the carriage.

You have a friend, you send him to dance with your wife, for you have commenced a system of concessions which will ruin you. You already dimly perceive the advantage of a friend.

Finally, you order the carriage. You wife gets in with concentrated rage, she hurls herself into a corner, covers her face with her hood, crosses her arms under her pelisse, and says not a word.

O husbands! Learn this fact; you may, at this fatal moment, repair and redeem everything: and never does the impetuosity of lovers who have been caressing each other the whole evening with flaming gaze fail to do it! Yes, you can bring her home in triumph, she has now nobody but you, you have one more chance, that of taking your wife by storm! But no, idiot, stupid and indifferent that you are, you ask her, "What is the matter?"

Axiom.—A husband should always know what is the matter with his wife, for she always knows what is not.

"I'm cold," she says.

"The ball was splendid."

"Pooh! nobody of distinction! People have the mania, nowadays, to invite all Paris into a hole. There were women even on the stairs: their gowns were horribly smashed, and mine is ruined."

"We had a good time."

"Ah, you men, you play and that's the whole of it. Once married, you care about as much for your wives as a lion does for the fine arts."

"How changed you are; you were so gay, so happy, so charming when we arrived."

"Oh, you never understand us women. I begged you to go home, and you left me there, as if a woman ever did anything without a reason. You are not without intelligence, but now and then you are so queer I don't know what you are thinking about."

Once upon this footing, the quarrel becomes more bitter. When you give your wife your hand to lift her from the carriage, you grasp a woman of wood: she gives you a "thank you" which puts you in the same rank as her servant. You understood your wife no better before than you do after the ball: you find it difficult to follow her, for instead of going up stairs, she flies up. The rupture is complete.

The chambermaid is involved in your disgrace: she is received with blunt No's and Yes's, as dry as Brussells rusks, which she swallows with a slanting glance at you. "Monsieur's always doing these things," she mutters.

You alone might have changed Madame's temper. She goes to bed; she has her revenge to take: you did not comprehend her. Now she does not comprehend you. She deposits herself on her side of the bed in the most hostile and offensive posture: she is wrapped up in her chemise, in her sack, in her night-cap, like a bale of clocks packed for the East Indies. She says neither good-night, nor good-day, nor dear, nor Adolphe: you don't exist, you are a bag of wheat.

Your Caroline, so enticing five hours before in this very chamber where she frisked about like an eel, is now a junk of lead. Were you the Tropical Zone in person, astride of the Equator, you could not melt the ice of this little personified Switzerland that pretends to be asleep, and who could freeze you from head to foot, if she liked. Ask her one hundred times what is the matter with her, Switzerland replies by an ultimatum, like the Diet or the Conference of London.

Nothing is the matter with her: she is tired: she is going to sleep.

The more you insist, the more she erects bastions of ignorance, the more she isolates herself by chevaux-de-frise. If you get impatient, Caroline begins to dream! You grumble, you are lost.

Axiom.—Inasmuch as women are always willing and able to explain their strong points, they leave us to guess at their weak ones.

Caroline will perhaps also condescend to assure you that she does not feel well. But she laughs in her night-cap when you have fallen asleep, and hurls imprecations upon your slumbering body.

WOMEN'S LOGIC.

You imagine you have married a creature endowed with reason: you are woefully mistaken, my friend.

Axiom.—Sensitive beings are not sensible beings.

Sentiment is not argument, reason is not pleasure, and pleasure is certainly not a reason.

"Oh! sir!" she says.

Reply "Ah! yes! Ah!" You must bring forth this "ah!" from the very depths of your thoracic cavern, as you rush in a rage from the house, or return, confounded, to your study.

Why? Now? Who has conquered, killed, overthrown you! Your wife's logic, which is not the logic of Aristotle, nor that of Ramus, nor that of Kant, nor that of Condillac, nor that of Robespierre, nor that of Napoleon: but which partakes of the character of all these logics, and which we must call the universal logic of women, the logic of English women as it is that of Italian women, of the women of Normandy and Brittany (ah, these last are unsurpassed!), of the women of Paris, in short, that of the women in the moon, if there are women in that nocturnal land, with which the women of the earth have an evident understanding, angels that they are!

The discussion began after breakfast. Discussions can never take place in a household save at this hour. A man could hardly have a discussion with his wife in bed, even if he wanted to: she has too many advantages over him, and can too easily reduce him to silence. On leaving the nuptial chamber with a pretty woman in it, a man is apt to be hungry, if he is young. Breakfast is usually a cheerful meal, and cheerfulness is not given to argument. In short, you do not open the business till you have had your tea or your coffee.

You have taken it into your head, for instance, to send your son to school. All fathers are hypocrites and are never willing to confess that their own flesh and blood is very troublesome when it walks about on two legs, lays its dare-devil hands on everything, and is everywhere at once like a frisky pollywog. Your son barks, mews, and sings; he breaks, smashes and soils the furniture, and furniture is dear; he makes toys of everything, he scatters your papers, and he cuts paper dolls out of the morning's newspaper before you have read it.

His mother says to him, referring to anything of yours: "Take it!" but in reference to anything of hers she says: "Take care!"

She cunningly lets him have your things that she may be left in peace. Her bad faith as a good mother seeks shelter behind her child, your son is her accomplice. Both are leagued against you like Robert Macaire and Bertrand against the subscribers to their joint stock company. The boy is an axe with which foraging excursions are performed in your domains. He goes either boldly or slyly to maraud in your wardrobe: he reappears caparisoned in the drawers you laid aside that morning, and brings to the light of day many articles condemned to solitary confinement. He brings the elegant Madame Fischtaminel, a friend whose good graces you cultivate, your girdle for checking corpulency, bits of cosmetic for dyeing your moustache, old waistcoats discolored at the arm-holes, stockings slightly soiled at the heels and somewhat yellow at the toes. It is quite impossible to remark that these stains are caused by the leather!

Your wife looks at your friend and laughs; you dare not be angry, so you laugh too, but what a laugh! The unfortunate all know that laugh.

Your son, moreover, gives you a cold sweat, if your razors happen to be out of their place. If you are angry, the little rebel laughs and shows his two rows of pearls: if you scold him, he cries. His mother rushes in! And what a mother she is! A mother who will detest you if you don't give him the razor! With women there is no middle ground; a man is either a monster or a model.

At certain times you perfectly understand Herod and his famous decrees relative to the Massacre of the Innocents, which have only been surpassed by those of the good Charles X!

Your wife has returned to her sofa, you walk up and down, and stop, and you boldly introduce the subject by this interjectional remark:

"Caroline, we must send Charles to boarding school."

29

"Charles cannot go to boarding school," she returns in a mild tone.

"Charles is six years old, the age at which a boy's education begins."

"In the first place," she replies, "it begins at seven. The royal princes are handed over to their governor by their governess when they are seven. That's the law and the prophets. I don't see why you shouldn't apply to the children of private people the rule laid down for the children of princes. Is your son more forward than theirs? The king of Rome—"

"The king of Rome is not a case in point."

"What! Is not the king of Rome the son of the Emperor? [Here she changes the subject.] Well, I declare, you accuse the Empress, do you? Why, Doctor Dubois himself was present, besides—"

"I said nothing of the kind."

"How you do interrupt, Adolphe."

"I say that the king of Rome [here you begin to raise your voice], the king of Rome, who was hardly four years old when he left France, is no example for us."

"That doesn't prevent the fact of the Duke de Bordeaux's having been placed in the hands of the Duke de Riviere, his tutor, at seven years." [Logic.]

"The case of the young Duke of Bordeaux is different."

"Then you confess that a boy can't be sent to school before he is seven years old?" she says with emphasis. [More logic.]

"No, my dear, I don't confess that at all. There is a great deal of difference between private and public education."

"That's precisely why I don't want to send Charles to school yet. He ought to be much stronger than he is, to go there."

"Charles is very strong for his age."

"Charles? That's the way with men! Why, Charles has a very weak constitution; he takes after you. [Here she changes from *tu* to *vous*.] But if you are determined to get rid of your son, why put him out to board, of course. I have noticed for some time that the dear child annoys you."

"Annoys me? The idea! But we are answerable for our children, are we not? It is time Charles' education was began: he is getting very bad habits here, he obeys no one, he thinks himself perfectly free to do as he likes, he hits everybody and nobody dares to hit him back. He ought to be placed in the midst of his equals, or he will grow up with the most detestable temper."

"Thank you: so I am bringing Charles up badly!"

"I did not say that: but you will always have excellent reasons for keeping him at home."

Here the *vous* becomes reciprocal and the discussion takes a bitter turn on both sides. Your wife is very willing to wound you by saying *vous*, but she feels cross when it becomes mutual.

"The long and the short of it is that you want to get my child away, you find that he is between us, you are jealous of your son, you want to tyrannize over me at your ease, and you sacrifice your boy! Oh, I am smart enough to see through you!"

"You make me out like Abraham with his knife! One would think there were no such things as schools! So the schools are empty; nobody sends their children to school!"

"You are trying to make me appear ridiculous," she retorts. "I know that there are schools well enough, but people don't send boys of six there, and Charles shall not start now."

"Don't get angry, my dear."

"As if I ever get angry! I am a woman and know how to suffer in silence."

"Come, let us reason together."

"You have talked nonsense enough."

"It is time that Charles should learn to read and write; later in life, he will find difficulties sufficient to disgust him."

Here, you talk for ten minutes without interruption, and you close with an appealing "Well?" armed with an intonation which suggests an interrogation point of the most crooked kind.

"Well!" she replies, "it is not yet time for Charles to go to school."

You have gained nothing at all.

"But, my dear, Monsieur Deschars certainly sent his little Julius to school at six years. Go and examine the schools and you will find lots of little boys of six there."

You talk for ten minutes more without the slightest interruption, and then you ejaculate another "Well?"

"Little Julius Deschars came home with chilblains," she says.

"But Charles has chilblains here."

"Never," she replies, proudly.

In a quarter of an hour, the main question is blocked by a side discussion on this point: "Has Charles had chilblains or not?"

You bandy contradictory allegations; you no longer believe each other; you must appeal to a third party.

Axiom.—Every household has its Court of Appeals which takes no notice of the merits, but judges matters of form only.

The nurse is sent for. She comes, and decides in favor of your wife. It is fully decided that Charles has never had chilblains.

Caroline glances triumphantly at you and utters these monstrous words: "There, you see Charles can't possibly go to school!"

You go out breathless with rage. There is no earthly means of convincing your wife that there is not the slightest reason for your son's not going to school in the fact that he has never had chilblains.

That evening, after dinner, you hear this atrocious creature finishing a long conversation with a woman with these words: "He wanted to send Charles to school, but I made him see that he would have to wait."

Some husbands, at a conjuncture like this, burst out before everybody; their wives take their revenge six weeks later, but the husbands gain this by it, that Charles is sent to school the very day he gets into any mischief. Other husbands break the crockery, and keep their rage to themselves. The knowing ones say nothing and bide their time.

A woman's logic is exhibited in this way upon the slightest occasion, about a promenade or the proper place to put a sofa. This logic is extremely simple, inasmuch as it consists in never expressing but one idea, that which contains the expression of their will. Like everything pertaining to female nature, this system may be resolved into two algebraic terms—Yes: no. There are also certain little movements of the head which mean so much that they may take the place of either.

THE JESUITISM OF WOMEN.

The most jesuitical Jesuit of Jesuits is yet a thousand times less jesuitical than the least jesuitical woman,—so you may judge what Jesuits women are! They are so jesuitical that the cunningest Jesuit himself could never guess to what extent of jesuitism a woman may go, for there are a thousand ways of being jesuitical, and a woman is such an adroit Jesuit, that she has the knack of being a Jesuit without having a jesuitical look. You can rarely, though you can sometimes, prove to a Jesuit that he is one: but try once to demonstrate to a woman that she acts or talks like a Jesuit. She would be cut to pieces rather than confess herself one.

She, a Jesuit! The very soul of honor and loyalty! She a Jesuit! What do you mean by "Jesuit?" She does not know what a Jesuit is: what is a Jesuit? She has never seen or heard of a Jesuit! It's you who are a Jesuit! And she proves with jesuitical demonstration that you are a subtle Jesuit.

Here is one of the thousand examples of a woman's jesuitism, and this example constitutes the most terrible of the petty troubles of married life; it is perhaps the most serious.

Induced by a desire the thousandth time expressed by Caroline, who complained that she had to go on foot or that she could not buy a new hat, a new parasol, a new dress, or any other article of dress, often enough:

That she could not dress her baby as a sailor, as a lancer, as an artilleryman of the National Guard, as a Highlander with naked legs and a cap and feather, in a jacket, in a roundabout, in a velvet sack, in boots, in trousers: that she could not buy him toys enough, nor mechanical moving mice and Noah's Arks enough:

That she could not return Madame Deschars or Madame de Fischtaminel their civilities, a ball, a party, a dinner: nor take a private box at the theatre, thus avoiding the necessity of sitting cheek by jowl with men who are either too polite or not enough so, and of calling a cab at the close of the performance; apropos of which she thus discourses:

"You think it cheaper, but you are mistaken: men are all the same! I soil my shoes, I spoil my hat, my shawl gets wet and my silk stockings get muddy. You economize twenty francs by not having a carriage,—no not twenty, sixteen, for your pay four for the cab—and you lose fifty francs' worth of dress, besides being wounded in your pride on seeing a faded bonnet on my head: you don't see why it's faded, but it's those horrid cabs. I say nothing of the annoyance of being tumbled and jostled by a crowd of men, for it seems you don't care for that!"

That she could not buy a piano instead of hiring one, nor keep up with the fashions; (there are some women, she says, who have all the new styles, but just think what they give in return! She would rather throw herself out of the window than imitate them! She loves you too much. Here she sheds tears. She does not understand such women). That she could not ride in the Champs Elysees, stretched out in her own carriage, like Madame de Fischtaminel. (There's a woman who understands life: and who has a well-taught, well-disciplined and very contented husband: his wife would go through fire and water for him!)

Finally, beaten in a thousand conjugal scenes, beaten by the most logical arguments (the late logicians Tripier and Merlin were nothing to her, as the preceding chapter has sufficiently shown you), beaten by the most tender caresses, by tears, by your own words turned against you, for under circumstances like these, a woman lies in wait in her house like a jaguar in the jungle; she does not appear to listen to you, or to heed you; but if a single word, a wish, a gesture, escapes you, she arms herself with it, she whets it to an edge, she brings it to bear upon you a hundred times over; beaten by such graceful tricks as "If you will do so and so, I will do this and that;" for women, in these cases, become greater bargainers than the Jews and Greeks (those, I mean, who sell perfumes and little girls), than the Arabs (those, I mean, who sell little boys and horses), greater higglers than the Swiss and the Genevese, than bankers, and, what is worse than all, than the Genoese!

Finally, beaten in a manner which may be called beaten, you determine to risk a certain portion of your capital in a business undertaking. One evening, at twilight, seated side by side, or some morning on awakening, while Caroline, half asleep, a pink bud in her white linen, her face smiling in her lace, is beside you, you say to her, "You want this, you say, or you want that: you told me this or you told me that:" in short, you hastily enumerate the numberless fancies by which she has over and over again broken your heart, for there is nothing more dreadful than to be unable to satisfy the desires of a beloved wife, and you close with these words:

"Well, my dear, an opportunity offers of quintupling a hundred thousand francs, and I have decided to make the venture."

She is wide awake now, she sits up in bed, and gives you a kiss, ah! this time, a real good one!

"You are a dear boy!" is her first word.

We will not mention her last, for it is an enormous and unpronounceable onomatope.

"Now," she says, "tell me all about it."

You try to explain the nature of the affair. But in the first place, women do not understand business, and in the next they do not wish to seem to understand it. Your dear, delighted Caroline says you were wrong to take her desires, her groans, her sighs for new dresses, in earnest. She is afraid of your venture, she is frightened at the directors, the shares, and above all at the running expenses, and doesn't exactly see where the dividend comes in.

Axiom.—Women are always afraid of things that have to be divided.

In short, Caroline suspects a trap: but she is delighted to know that she can have her carriage, her box, the numerous styles of dress for her baby, and the rest. While dissuading you from engaging in the speculation, she is visibly glad to see you investing your money in it.

FIRST PERIOD.—"Oh, I am the happiest woman on the face of the earth! Adolphe has just gone into the most splendid venture. I am going to have a carriage, oh! ever so much handsomer than Madame de Fischtaminel's; hers is out of fashion. Mine will have curtains with fringes. My horses will be mouse-colored, hers are bay,—they are as common as coppers."

"What is this venture, madame?"

"Oh, it's splendid—the stock is going up; he explained it to me before he went into it, for Adolphe never does anything without consulting me."

"You are very fortunate."

"Marriage would be intolerable without entire confidence, and Adolphe tells me everything."

Thus, Adolphe, you are the best husband in Paris, you are adorable, you are a man of genius, you are all heart, an angel. You are petted to an uncomfortable degree. You bless the marriage tie. Caroline extols men, calling them "kings of creation," women were made for them, man is naturally generous, and matrimony is a delightful institution.

For three, sometimes six, months, Caroline executes the most brilliant concertos and solos upon this delicious theme: "I shall be rich! I shall have a thousand a month for my dress: I am going to keep my carriage!"

If your son is alluded to, it is merely to ask about the school to which he shall be sent.

SECOND PERIOD.—"Well, dear, how is your business getting on?—What has become of it?—How about that speculation which was to give me a carriage, and other things?—It is high time that affair should come to something.—It is a good while cooking.—When *will* it begin to pay? Is the stock going up?—There's nobody like you for hitting upon ventures that never amount to anything."

One day she says to you, "Is there really an affair?"

If you mention it eight or ten months after, she returns:

"Ah! Then there really *is* an affair!"

This woman, whom you thought dull, begins to show signs of extraordinary wit, when her object is to make fun of you. During this period, Caroline maintains a compromising silence when people speak of you, or else she speaks disparagingly of men in general: "Men are not what they seem: to find them out you must try them."

"Marriage has its good and its bad points." "Men never can finish anything."

THIRD PERIOD.—*Catastrophe.*—This magnificent affair which was to yield five hundred per cent, in which the most cautious, the best informed persons took part—peers, deputies, bankers—all of them Knights of the Legion of Honor—this venture has been obliged to liquidate! The most sanguine expect to get ten per cent of their capital back. You are discouraged.

Caroline has often said to you, "Adolphe, what is the matter? Adolphe, there is something wrong."

Finally, you acquaint Caroline with the fatal result: she begins by consoling you.

"One hundred thousand francs lost! We shall have to practice the strictest economy," you imprudently add.

The jesuitism of woman bursts out at this word "economy." It sets fire to the magazine.

"Ah! that's what comes of speculating! How is it that *you, ordinarily so prudent*, could go and risk a hundred thousand francs! *You know I was against it from the beginning!* BUT YOU WOULD NOT LISTEN TO ME!"

Upon this, the discussion grows bitter.

You are good for nothing—you have no business capacity; women alone take clear views of things. You have risked your children's bread, though she tried to dissuade you from it.—You cannot say it was for her. Thank God, she has nothing to reproach herself with. A hundred times a month she alludes to your disaster: "If my husband had not thrown away his money in such and such a scheme, I could have had this and that." "The next time you want to go into an affair, perhaps you'll consult me!" Adolphe is accused and convicted of having foolishly lost one hundred thousand francs, without an object in view, like a dolt, and without having consulted his wife. Caroline advises her friends not to marry. She complains of the incapacity of men who squander the fortunes of their wives. Caroline is vindictive, she makes herself generally disagreeable. Pity Adolphe! Lament, ye husbands! O bachelors, rejoice and be exceeding glad!

MEMORIES AND REGRETS.

After several years of wedded life, your love has become so placid, that Caroline sometimes tries, in the evening, to wake you up by various little coquettish phrases. There is about you a certain calmness and tranquillity which always exasperates a lawful wife. Women see in it a sort of insolence: they look upon the indifference of happiness as the fatuity of confidence, for of course they never imagine their inestimable equalities can be regarded with disdain: their virtue is therefore enraged at being so cordially trusted in.

In this situation, which is what every couple must come to, and which both husband and wife must expect, no husband dares confess that the constant repetition of the same dish has become wearisome; but his appetite certainly requires the condiments of dress, the ideas excited by absence, the stimulus of an imaginary rivalry.

In short, at this period, you walk very comfortably with your wife on your arm, without pressing hers against your heart with the solicitous and watchful cohesion of a miser grasping his treasure. You gaze carelessly round upon the curiosities in the street, leading your wife in a loose and distracted way, as if you were towing a Norman scow. Come now, be frank! If, on passing your wife, an admirer were gently to press her, accidentally or purposely, would you have the slightest desire to discover his motives? Besides, you say, no woman would seek to bring about a quarrel for such a trifle. Confess this, too, that the expression "such a trifle" is exceedingly flattering to both of you.

You are in this position, but you have as yet proceeded no farther. Still, you have a horrible thought which you bury in the depths of your heart and conscience: Caroline has not come up to your expectations. Caroline has imperfections, which, during the high tides of the honey-moon, were concealed under the water, but which the ebb of the gall-moon has laid bare. You have several times run against these breakers, your hopes have been often shipwrecked upon them, more than once your desires—those of a young marrying man—(where, alas, is that time!) have seen their richly laden gondolas go to pieces there: the flower of the cargo went to the bottom, the ballast of the marriage remained. In short, to make use of a colloquial expression, as you talk over your marriage with yourself you say, as you look at Caroline, *"She is not what I took her to be!"*

Some evening, at a ball, in society, at a friend's house, no matter where, you meet a sublime young woman, beautiful, intellectual and kind: with a soul, oh! a soul of celestial purity, and of miraculous beauty! Yes, there is that unchangeable oval cut of face, those features which time will never impair, that graceful and thoughtful brow. The unknown is rich, well-educated, of noble birth: she will always be what she should be, she knows when to shine, when to remain in the background: she appears in all her glory and power, the being you have dreamed of, your wife that should have been, she whom you feel you could love forever. She would always have flattered your little vanities, she would understand and admirably serve your interests. She is tender and gay, too, this young lady who reawakens all your better feelings, who rekindles your slumbering desires.

You look at Caroline with gloomy despair, and here are the phantom-like thoughts which tap, with wings of a bat, the beak of a vulture, the body of a death's-head moth, upon the walls of the palace in which, enkindled by desire, glows your brain like a lamp of gold:

FIRST STANZA. Ah, dear me, why did I get married? Fatal idea! I allowed myself to be caught by a small amount of cash. And is it really over? Cannot I have another wife? Ah, the Turks manage things better! It is plain enough that the author of the Koran lived in the desert!

SECOND STANZA. My wife is sick, she sometimes coughs in the morning. If it is the design of Providence to remove her from the world, let it be speedily done for her sake and for mine. The angel has lived long enough.

THIRD STANZA. I am a monster! Caroline is the mother of my children!

You go home, that night, in a carriage with your wife: you think her perfectly horrible: she speaks to you, but you answer in monosyllables. She says, "What is the matter?" and you answer, "Nothing." She coughs, you advise her to see the doctor in the morning. Medicine has its hazards.

FOURTH STANZA. I have been told that a physician, poorly paid by
the heirs of his deceased patient, imprudently exclaimed, "What!
they cut down my bill, when they owe me forty thousand a year." *I*
would not haggle over fees!

"Caroline," you say to her aloud, "you must take care of yourself;
cross your shawl, be prudent, my darling angel."

Your wife is delighted with you since you seem to take such an
interest in her. While she is preparing to retire, you lie stretched out
upon the sofa. You contemplate the divine apparition which opens
to you the ivory portals of your castles in the air. Delicious ecstasy!
'Tis the sublime young woman that you see before you! She is as
white as the sail of the treasure-laden galleon as it enters the harbor
of Cadiz. Your wife, happy in your admiration, now understands
your former taciturnity. You still see, with closed eyes, the sublime
young woman; she is the burden of your thoughts, and you say
aloud:

FIFTH AND LAST STANZA. Divine! Adorable! Can there be
another woman like her? Rose of Night! Column of ivory! Celestial
maiden! Morning and Evening Star!

Everyone says his prayers; you have said four.

The next morning, your wife is delightful, she coughs no more, she
has no need of a doctor; if she dies, it will be of good health; you
launched four maledictions upon her, in the name of your sublime
young woman, and four times she blessed you for it. Caroline does
not know that in the depths of your heart there wriggles a little red
fish like a crocodile, concealed beneath conjugal love like the other
would be hid in a basin.

A few days before, your wife had spoken of you in rather equivocal
terms to Madame de Fischtaminel: your fair friend comes to visit her,
and Caroline compromises you by a long and humid gaze; she
praises you and says she never was happier.

You rush out in a rage, you are beside yourself, and are glad to meet
a friend, that you may work off your bile.

"Don't you ever marry, George; it's better to see your heirs carrying
away your furniture while the death-rattle is in your throat, better to

go through an agony of two hours without a drop to cool your tongue, better to be assassinated by inquiries about your will by a nurse like the one in Henry Monnier's terrible picture of a 'Bachelor's Last Moments!' Never marry under any pretext!"

Fortunately you see the sublime young woman no more. You are saved from the tortures to which a criminal passion was leading you. You fall back again into the purgatory of your married bliss; but you begin to be attentive to Madame de Fischtaminel, with whom you were dreadfully in love, without being able to get near her, while you were a bachelor.

OBSERVATIONS.

When you have arrived at this point in the latitude or longitude of the matrimonial ocean, there appears a slight chronic, intermittent affection, not unlike the toothache. Here, I see, you stop me to ask, "How are we to find the longitude in this sea? When can a husband be sure he has attained this nautical point? And can the danger be avoided?"

You may arrive at this point, look you, as easily after ten months as ten years of wedlock; it depends upon the speed of the vessel, its style of rigging, upon the trade winds, the force of the currents, and especially upon the composition of the crew. You have this advantage over the mariner, that he has but one method of calculating his position, while husbands have at least a thousand of reckoning theirs.

EXAMPLE: Caroline, your late darling, your late treasure, who is now merely your humdrum wife, leans much too heavily upon your arm while walking on the boulevard, or else says it is much more elegant not to take your arm at all;

Or else she notices men, older or younger as the case may be, dressed with more or less taste, whereas she formerly saw no one whatever, though the sidewalk was black with hats and traveled by more boots than slippers;

Or, when you come home, she says, "It's no one but my husband:" instead of saying "Ah! 'tis Adolphe!" as she used to say with a gesture, a look, an accent which caused her admirers to think, "Well, here's a happy woman at last!" This last exclamation of a woman is suitable for two eras,—first, while she is sincere; second, while she is hypocritical, with her "Ah! 'tis Adolphe!" When she exclaims, "It's only my husband," she no longer deigns to play a part.

Or, if you come home somewhat late—at eleven, or at midnight— you find her—snoring! Odious symptom!

Or else she puts on her stockings in your presence. Among English couples, this never happens but once in a lady's married life; the next day she leaves for the Continent with some captain or other, and no longer thinks of putting on her stockings at all.

Or else—but let us stop here.

This is intended for the use of mariners and husbands who are weatherwise.

THE MATRIMONIAL GADFLY.

Very well! In this degree of longitude, not far from a tropical sign upon the name of which good taste forbids us to make a jest at once coarse and unworthy of this thoughtful work, a horrible little annoyance appears, ingeniously called the Matrimonial Gadfly, the most provoking of all gnats, mosquitoes, blood-suckers, fleas and scorpions, for no net was ever yet invented that could keep it off. The gadfly does not immediately sting you; it begins by buzzing in your ears, and *you do not at first know what it is.*

Thus, apropos of nothing, in the most natural way in the world, Caroline says: "Madame Deschars had a lovely dress on, yesterday."

"She is a woman of taste," returns Adolphe, though he is far from thinking so.

"Her husband gave it to her," resumes Caroline, with a shrug of her shoulders.

"Ah!"

"Yes, a four hundred franc dress! It's the very finest quality of velvet."

"Four hundred francs!" cries Adolphe, striking the attitude of the apostle Thomas.

"But then there are two extra breadths and enough for a high waist!"

"Monsieur Deschars does things on a grand scale," replies Adolphe, taking refuge in a jest.

"All men don't pay such attentions to their wives," says Caroline, curtly.

"What attentions?"

"Why, Adolphe, thinking of extra breadths and of a waist to make the dress good again, when it is no longer fit to be worn low in the neck."

Adolphe says to himself, "Caroline wants a dress."

Poor man!

Some time afterward, Monsieur Deschars furnishes his wife's chamber anew. Then he has his wife's diamonds set in the prevailing fashion. Monsieur Deschars never goes out without his wife, and never allows his wife to go out without offering her his arm.

If you bring Caroline anything, no matter what, it is never equal to what Monsieur Deschars has done. If you allow yourself the slightest gesture or expression a little livelier than usual, if you speak a little bit loud, you hear the hissing and viper-like remark:

"You wouldn't see Monsieur Deschars behaving like this! Why don't you take Monsieur Deschars for a model?"

In short, this idiotic Monsieur Deschars is forever looming up in your household on every conceivable occasion.

The expression—"Do you suppose Monsieur Deschars ever allows himself" —is a sword of Damocles, or what is worse, a Damocles pin: and your self-love is the cushion into which your wife is constantly sticking it, pulling it out, and sticking it in again, under a variety of unforeseen pretexts, at the same time employing the most winning terms of endearment, and with the most agreeable little ways.

Adolphe, stung till he finds himself tattooed, finally does what is done by police authorities, by officers of government, by military tacticians. He casts his eye on Madame de Fischtaminel, who is still young, elegant and a little bit coquettish, and places her (this had been the rascal's intention for some time) like a blister upon Caroline's extremely ticklish skin.

O you, who often exclaim, "I don't know what is the matter with my wife!" you will kiss this page of transcendent philosophy, for you will find in it *the key to every woman's character*! But as to knowing women as well as I know them, it will not be knowing them much; they don't know themselves! In fact, as you well know, God was Himself mistaken in the only one that He attempted to manage and to whose manufacture He had given personal attention.

Caroline is very willing to sting Adolphe at all hours, but this privilege of letting a wasp off now and then upon one's consort (the legal term), is exclusively reserved to the wife. Adolphe is a monster if he starts off a single fly at Caroline. On her part, it is a delicious joke, a new jest to enliven their married life, and one dictated by the purest intentions; while on Adolphe's part, it is a piece of cruelty worthy a Carib, a disregard of his wife's heart, and a deliberate plan to give her pain. But that is nothing.

"So you are really in love with Madame de Fischtaminel?" Caroline asks. "What is there so seductive in the mind or the manners of the spider?"

"Why, Caroline—"

"Oh, don't undertake to deny your eccentric taste," she returns, checking a negation on Adolphe's lips. "I have long seen that you prefer that Maypole [Madame de Fischtaminel is thin] to me. Very well! go on; you will soon see the difference."

Do you understand? You cannot suspect Caroline of the slightest inclination for Monsieur Deschars, a low, fat, red-faced man, formerly a notary, while you are in love with Madame de Fischtaminel! Then Caroline, the Caroline whose simplicity caused you such agony, Caroline who has become familiar with society, Caroline becomes acute and witty: you have two gadflies instead of one.

The next day she asks you, with a charming air of interest, "How are you coming on with Madame de Fischtaminel?"

When you go out, she says: "Go and drink something calming, my dear." For, in their anger with a rival, all women, duchesses even, will use invectives, and even venture into the domain of Billingsgate; they make an offensive weapon of anything and everything.

To try to convince Caroline that she is mistaken and that you are indifferent to Madame de Fischtaminel, would cost you dear. This is a blunder that no sensible man commits; he would lose his power and spike his own guns.

Oh! Adolphe, you have arrived unfortunately at that season so ingeniously called the *Indian Summer of Marriage*.

You must now—pleasing task!—win your wife, your Caroline, over again, seize her by the waist again, and become the best of husbands by trying to guess at things to please her, so as to act according to her whims instead of according to your will. This is the whole question henceforth.

HARD LABOR.

Let us admit this, which, in our opinion, is a truism made as good as new:

Axiom.—Most men have some of the wit required by a difficult position, when they have not the whole of it.

As for those husbands who are not up to their situation, it is impossible to consider their case here: without any struggle whatever they simply enter the numerous class of the *Resigned*.

Adolphe says to himself: "Women are children: offer them a lump of sugar, and you will easily get them to dance all the dances that greedy children dance; but you must always have a sugar plum in hand, hold it up pretty high, and—take care that their fancy for sweetmeats does not leave them. Parisian women—and Caroline is one—are very vain, and as for their voracity—don't speak of it. Now you cannot govern men and make friends of them, unless you work upon them through their vices, and flatter their passions: my wife is mine!"

Some days afterward, during which Adolphe has been unusually attentive to his wife, he discourses to her as follows:

"Caroline, dear, suppose we have a bit of fun: you'll put on your new gown—the one like Madame Deschars!—and we'll go to see a farce at the Varieties."

This kind of proposition always puts a wife in the best possible humor. So away you go! Adolphe has ordered a dainty little dinner for two, at Borrel's *Rocher de Cancale*.

"As we are going to the Varieties, suppose we dine at the tavern," exclaims Adolphe, on the boulevard, with the air of a man suddenly struck by a generous idea.

Caroline, delighted with this appearance of good fortune, enters a little parlor where she finds the cloth laid and that neat little service set, which Borrel places at the disposal of those who are rich enough to pay for the quarters intended for the great ones of the earth, who make themselves small for an hour.

Women eat little at a formal dinner: their concealed harness hampers them, they are laced tightly, and they are in the presence of women whose eyes and whose tongues are equally to be dreaded. They prefer fancy eating to good eating, then: they will suck a lobster's claw, swallow a quail or two, punish a woodcock's wing, beginning with a bit of fresh fish, flavored by one of those sauces which are the glory of French cooking. France is everywhere sovereign in matters of taste: in painting, fashions, and the like. Gravy is the triumph of taste, in cookery. So that grisettes, shopkeepers' wives and duchesses are delighted with a tasty little dinner washed down with the choicest wines, of which, however, they drink but little, the whole concluded by fruit such as can only be had at Paris; and especially delighted when they go to the theatre to digest the little dinner, and listen, in a comfortable box, to the nonsense uttered upon the stage, and to that whispered in their ears to explain it. But then the bill of the restaurant is one hundred francs, the box costs thirty, the carriage, dress, gloves, bouquet, as much more. This gallantry amounts to the sum of one hundred and sixty francs, which is hard upon four thousand francs a month, if you go often to the Comic, the Italian, or the Grand, Opera. Four thousand francs a month is the interest of a capital of two millions. But then the honor of being a husband is fully worth the price!

Caroline tells her friends things which she thinks exceedingly flattering, but which cause a sagacious husband to make a wry face.

"Adolphe has been delightful for some time past. I don't know what I have done to deserve so much attention, but he overpowers me. He gives value to everything by those delicate ways which have such an effect upon us women. After taking me Monday to the *Rocher de Cancale* to dine, he declared that Very was as good a cook as Borrel, and he gave me the little party of pleasure that I told you of all over again, presenting me at dessert with a ticket for the opera. They sang 'William Tell,' which, you know, is my craze."

"You are lucky indeed," returns Madame Deschars with evident jealousy.

"Still, a wife who discharges all her duties, deserves such luck, it seems to me."

When this terrible sentiment falls from the lips of a married woman, it is clear that she *does her duty*, after the manner of school-boys, for the reward she expects. At school, a prize is the object: in marriage, a shawl or a piece of jewelry. No more love, then!

"As for me,"—Madame Deschars is piqued—"I am reasonable. Deschars committed such follies once, but I put a stop to it. You see, my dear, we have two children, and I confess that one or two hundred francs are quite a consideration for me, as the mother of a family."

"Dear me, madame," says Madame de Fischtaminel, "it's better that our husbands should have cosy little times with us than with—"

"Deschars!—" suddenly puts in Madame Deschars, as she gets up and says good-bye.

The individual known as Deschars (a man nullified by his wife) does not hear the end of the sentence, by which he might have learned that a man may spend his money with other women.

Caroline, flattered in every one of her vanities, abandons herself to the pleasures of pride and high living, two delicious capital sins. Adolphe is gaining ground again, but alas! (this reflection is worth a whole sermon in Lent) sin, like all pleasure, contains a spur. Vice is like an Autocrat, and let a single harsh fold in a rose-leaf irritate it, it forgets a thousand charming bygone flatteries. With Vice a man's course must always be crescendo!—and forever.

Axiom.—Vice, Courtiers, Misfortune and Love, care only for the PRESENT.

At the end of a period of time difficult to determine, Caroline looks in the glass, at dessert, and notices two or three pimples blooming upon her cheeks, and upon the sides, lately so pure, of her nose. She is out of humor at the theatre, and you do not know why, you, so proudly striking an attitude in your cravat, you, displaying your figure to the best advantage, as a complacent man should.

A few days after, the dressmaker arrives. She tries on a gown, she exerts all her strength, but cannot make the hooks and eyes meet. The waiting maid is called. After a two horse-power pull, a regular thirteenth labor of Hercules, a hiatus of two inches manifests itself.

The inexorable dressmaker cannot conceal from Caroline the fact that her form is altered. Caroline, the aerial Caroline, threatens to become like Madame Deschars. In vulgar language, she is getting stout. The maid leaves her in a state of consternation.

"What! am I to have, like that fat Madame Deschars, cascades of flesh a la Rubens! That Adolphe is an awful scoundrel. Oh, I see, he wants to make me an old mother Gigogne, and destroy my powers of fascination!"

Thenceforward Caroline is willing to go to the opera, she accepts two seats in a box, but she considers it very distingue to eat sparingly, and declines the dainty dinners of her husband.

"My dear," she says, "a well-bred woman should not go often to these places; you may go once for a joke; but as for making a habitual thing of it—fie, for shame!"

Borrel and Very, those masters of the art, lose a thousand francs a day by not having a private entrance for carriages. If a coach could glide under an archway, and go out by another door, after leaving its fair occupants on the threshold of an elegant staircase, how many of them would bring the landlord fine, rich, solid old fellows for customers!

Axiom.—Vanity is the death of good living.

Caroline very soon gets tired of the theatre, and the devil alone can tell the cause of her disgust. Pray excuse Adolphe! A husband is not the devil.

Fully one-third of the women of Paris are bored by the theatre. Many of them are tired to death of music, and go to the opera for the singers merely, or rather to notice the difference between them in point of execution. What supports the theatre is this: the women are a spectacle before and after the play. Vanity alone will pay the exorbitant price of forty francs for three hours of questionable pleasure, in a bad atmosphere and at great expense, without counting the colds caught in going out. But to exhibit themselves, to see and be seen, to be the observed of five hundred observers! What a glorious mouthful! as Rabelais would say.

To obtain this precious harvest, garnered by self-love, a woman must be looked at. Now a woman with her husband is very little looked at. Caroline is chagrined to see the audience entirely taken up with women who are *not* with their husbands, with eccentric women, in short. Now, as the very slight return she gets from her efforts, her dresses, and her attitudes, does not compensate, in her eyes, for her fatigue, her display and her weariness, it is very soon the same with the theatre as it was with the good cheer; high living made her fat, the theatre is making her yellow.

Here Adolphe—or any other man in Adolphe's place—resembles a certain Languedocian peasant who suffered agonies from an agacin, or, in French, corn,—but the term in Lanquedoc is so much prettier, don't you think so? This peasant drove his foot at each step two inches into the sharpest stones along the roadside, saying to the agacin, "Devil take you! Make me suffer again, will you?"

"Upon my word," says Adolphe, profoundly disappointed, the day when he receives from his wife a refusal, "I should like very much to know what would please you!"

Caroline looks loftily down upon her husband, and says, after a pause worthy of an actress, "I am neither a Strasburg goose nor a giraffe!"

"'Tis true, I might lay out four thousand francs a month to better effect," returns Adolphe.

"What do you mean?"

"With the quarter of that sum, presented to estimable burglars, youthful jail-birds and honorable criminals, I might become somebody, a Man in the Blue Cloak on a small scale; and then a young woman is proud of her husband," Adolphe replies.

This answer is the grave of love, and Caroline takes it in very bad part. An explanation follows. This must be classed among the thousand pleasantries of the following chapter, the title of which ought to make lovers smile as well as husbands. If there are yellow rays of light, why should there not be whole days of this extremely matrimonial color?

FORCED SMILES.

On your arrival in this latitude, you enjoy numerous little scenes, which, in the grand opera of marriage, represent the intermezzos, and of which the following is a type:

You are one evening alone after dinner, and you have been so often alone already that you feel a desire to say sharp little things to each other, like this, for instance:

"Take care, Caroline," says Adolphe, who has not forgotten his many vain efforts to please her. "I think your nose has the impertinence to redden at home quite well as at the restaurant."

"This is not one of your amiable days!"

General Rule.—No man has ever yet discovered the way to give friendly advice to any woman, not even to his own wife.

"Perhaps it's because you are laced too tight. Women make themselves sick that way."

The moment a man utters these words to a woman, no matter whom, that woman,—who knows that stays will bend,—seizes her corset by the lower end, and bends it out, saying, with Caroline:

"Look, you can get your hand in! I never lace tight."

"Then it must be your stomach."

"What has the stomach got to do with the nose?"

"The stomach is a centre which communicates with all the organs."

"So the nose is an organ, is it?"

"Yes."

"Your organ is doing you a poor service at this moment." She raises her eyes and shrugs her shoulders. "Come, Adolphe, what have I done?"

"Nothing. I'm only joking, and I am unfortunate enough not to please you," returns Adolphe, smiling.

"My misfortune is being your wife! Oh, why am I not somebody else's!"

"That's what *I* say!"

"If I were, and if I had the innocence to say to you, like a coquette who wishes to know how far she has got with a man, 'the redness of my nose really gives me anxiety,' you would look at me in the glass with all the affectations of an ape, and would reply, 'O madame, you do yourself an injustice; in the first place, nobody sees it: besides, it harmonizes with your complexion; then again we are all so after dinner!' and from this you would go on to flatter me. Do I ever tell you that you are growing fat, that you are getting the color of a stone-cutter, and that I prefer thin and pale men?"

They say in London, "Don't touch the axe!" In France we ought to say, "Don't touch a woman's nose."

"And all this about a little extra natural vermilion!" exclaims Adolphe. "Complain about it to Providence, whose office it is to put a little more color in one place than another, not to me, who loves you, who desires you to be perfect, and who merely says to you, take care!"

"You love me too much, then, for you've been trying, for some time past, to find disagreeable things to say to me. You want to run me down under the pretext of making me perfect—people said I *was* perfect, five years ago."

"I think you are better than perfect, you are stunning!"

"With too much vermilion?"

Adolphe, who sees the atmosphere of the north pole upon his wife's face, sits down upon a chair by her side. Caroline, unable decently to go away, gives her gown a sort of flip on one side, as if to produce a separation. This motion is performed by some women with a provoking impertinence: but it has two significations; it is, as whist players would say, either a signal *for trumps* or a *renounce*. At this time, Caroline renounces.

"What is the matter?" says Adolphe.

"Will you have a glass of sugar and water?" asks Caroline, busying herself about your health, and assuming the part of a servant.

"What for?"

"You are not amiable while digesting, you must be in pain. Perhaps you would like a drop of brandy in your sugar and water? The doctor spoke of it as an excellent remedy."

"How anxious you are about my stomach!"

"It's a centre, it communicates with the other organs, it will act upon your heart, and through that perhaps upon your tongue."

Adolphe gets up and walks about without saying a word, but he reflects upon the acuteness which his wife is acquiring: he sees her daily gaining in strength and in acrimony: she is getting to display an art in vexation and a military capacity for disputation which reminds him of Charles XII and the Russians. Caroline, during this time, is busy with an alarming piece of mimicry: she looks as if she were going to faint.

"Are you sick?" asks Adolphe, attacked in his generosity, the place where women always have us.

"It makes me sick at my stomach, after dinner, to see a man going back and forth so, like the pendulum of a clock. But it's just like you: you are always in a fuss about something. You are a queer set: all men are more or less cracked."

Adolphe sits down by the fire opposite to his wife, and remains there pensive: marriage appears to him like an immense dreary plain, with its crop of nettles and mullen stalks.

"What, are you pouting?" asks Caroline, after a quarter of an hour's observation of her husband's countenance.

"No, I am meditating," replied Adolphe.

"Oh, what an infernal temper you've got!" she returns, with a shrug of the shoulders. "Is it for what I said about your stomach, your shape and your digestion? Don't you see that I was only paying you back for your vermilion? You'll make me think that men are as vain as women. [Adolphe remains frigid.] It is really quite kind in you to take our qualities. [Profound silence.] I made a joke and you got angry [she looks at Adolphe], for you are angry. I am not like you: I cannot bear the idea of having given you pain! Nevertheless, it's an idea that a man never would have had, that of attributing your impertinence to something wrong in your digestion. It's not my Dolph, it's his stomach that was bold enough to speak. I did not know you were a ventriloquist, that's all."

Caroline looks at Adolphe and smiles: Adolphe is as stiff as if he were glued.

"No, he won't laugh! And, in your jargon, you call this having character. Oh, how much better we are!"

She goes and sits down in Adolphe's lap, and Adolphe cannot help smiling. This smile, extracted as if by a steam engine, Caroline has been on the watch for, in order to make a weapon of it.

"Come, old fellow, confess that you are wrong," she says. "Why pout? Dear me, I like you just as you are: in my eyes you are as slender as when I married you, and slenderer perhaps."

"Caroline, when people get to deceive themselves in these little matters, where one makes concessions and the other does not get angry, do you know what it means?"

"What does it mean?" asks Caroline, alarmed at Adolphe's dramatic attitude.

"That they love each other less."

"Oh! you monster, I understand you: you were angry so as to make me believe you loved me!"

Alas! let us confess it, Adolphe tells the truth in the only way he can—by a laugh.

"Why give me pain?" she says. "If I am wrong in anything, isn't it better to tell me of it kindly, than brutally to say [here she raises her voice], 'Your nose is getting red!' No, that is not right! To please you,

I will use an expression of the fair Fischtaminel, 'It's not the act of a gentleman!'"

Adolphe laughs and pays the expenses of the reconciliation; but instead of discovering therein what will please Caroline and what will attach her to him, he finds out what attaches him to her.

NOSOGRAPHY OF THE VILLA.

Is it advantageous for a man not to know what will please his wife after their marriage? Some women (this still occurs in the country) are innocent enough to tell promptly what they want and what they like. But in Paris, nearly every woman feels a kind of enjoyment in seeing a man wistfully obedient to her heart, her desires, her caprices—three expressions for the same thing!—and anxiously going round and round, half crazy and desperate, like a dog that has lost his master.

They call this *being loved*, poor things! And a good many of them say to themselves, as did Caroline, "How will he manage?"

Adolphe has come to this. In this situation of things, the worthy and excellent Deschars, that model of the citizen husband, invites the couple known as Adolphe and Caroline to help him and his wife inaugurate a delightful country house. It is an opportunity that the Deschars have seized upon, the folly of a man of letters, a charming villa upon which he lavished one hundred thousand francs and which has been sold at auction for eleven thousand. Caroline has a new dress to air, or a hat with a weeping willow plume—things which a tilbury will set off to a charm. Little Charles is left with his grandmother. The servants have a holiday. The youthful pair start beneath the smile of a blue sky, flecked with milk-while clouds merely to heighten the effect. They breathe the pure air, through which trots the heavy Norman horse, animated by the influence of spring. They soon reach Marnes, beyond Ville d'Avray, where the Deschars are spreading themselves in a villa copied from one at Florence, and surrounded by Swiss meadows, though without all the objectionable features of the Alps.

"Dear me! what a delightful thing a country house like this must be!" exclaims Caroline, as she walks in the admirable wood that skirts Marnes and Ville d'Avray. "It makes your eyes as happy as if they had a heart in them."

Caroline, having no one to take but Adolphe, takes Adolphe, who becomes her Adolphe again. And then you should see her run about like a fawn, and act once more the sweet, pretty, innocent, adorable school-girl that she was! Her braids come down! She takes off her bonnet, and holds it by the strings! She is young, pink and white again. Her eyes smile, her mouth is a pomegranate endowed with sensibility, with a sensibility which seems quite fresh.

"So a country house would please you very much, would it, darling?" says Adolphe, clasping Caroline round the waist, and noticing that she leans upon him as if to show the flexibility of her form.

"What, will you be such a love as to buy me one? But remember, no extravagance! Seize an opportunity like the Deschars."

"To please you and to find out what is likely to give you pleasure, such is the constant study of your own Dolph."

They are alone, at liberty to call each other their little names of endearment, and run over the whole list of their secret caresses.

"Does he really want to please his little girly?" says Caroline, resting her head on the shoulder of Adolphe, who kisses her forehead, saying to himself, "Gad! I've got her now!"

Axiom.—When a husband and a wife have got each other, the devil only knows which has got the other.

The young couple are captivating, whereupon the stout Madame Deschars gives utterance to a remark somewhat equivocal for her, usually so stern, prudish and devout.

"Country air has one excellent property: it makes husbands very amiable."

M. Deschars points out an opportunity for Adolphe to seize. A house is to be sold at Ville d'Avray, for a song, of course. Now, the country house is a weakness peculiar to the inhabitant of Paris. This weakness, or disease, has its course and its cure. Adolphe is a husband, but not a doctor. He buys the house and takes possession with Caroline, who has become once more his Caroline, his Carola, his fawn, his treasure, his girly girl.

The following alarming symptoms now succeed each other with frightful rapidity: a cup of milk, baptized, costs five sous; when it is anhydrous, as the chemists say, ten sous. Meat costs more at Sevres than at Paris, if you carefully examine the qualities. Fruit cannot be had at any price. A fine pear costs more in the country than in the (anhydrous!) garden that blooms in Chevet's window.

Before being able to raise fruit for oneself, from a Swiss meadow measuring two square yards, surrounded by a few green trees which look as if they were borrowed from the scenic illusions of a theatre, the most rural authorities, being consulted on the point, declare that you must spend a great deal of money, and—wait five years! Vegetables dash out of the husbandman's garden to reappear at the city market. Madame Deschars, who possesses a gate-keeper that is at the same time a gardener, confesses that the vegetables raised on her land, beneath her glass frames, by dint of compost and top-soil, cost her twice as much as those she used to buy at Paris, of a woman who had rent and taxes to pay, and whose husband was an elector. Despite the efforts and pledges of the gate-keeper-gardener, early peas and things at Paris are a month in advance of those in the country.

From eight in the evening to eleven our couple don't know what to do, on account of the insipidity of the neighbors, their small ideas, and the questions of self-love which arise out of the merest trifles.

Monsieur Deschars remarks, with that profound knowledge of figures which distinguishes the ex-notary, that the cost of going to Paris and back, added to the interest of the cost of his villa, to the taxes, wages of the gate-keeper and his wife, are equal to a rent of three thousand francs a year. He does not see how he, an ex-notary, allowed himself to be so caught! For he has often drawn up leases of chateaux with parks and out-houses, for three thousand a year.

It is agreed by everybody in the parlor of Madame Deschars, that a country house, so far from being a pleasure, is an unmitigated nuisance.

"I don't see how they sell a cabbage for one sou at market, which has to be watered every day from its birth to the time you eat it," says Caroline.

"The way to get along in the country," replies a little retired grocer, "is to stay there, to live there, to become country-folks, and then everything changes."

On going home, Caroline says to her poor Adolphe, "What an idea that was of yours, to buy a country house! The best way to do about the country is to go there on visits to other people."

Adolphe remembers an English proverb, which says, "Don't have a newspaper or a country seat of your own: there are plenty of idiots who will have them for you."

"Bah!" returns Adolph, who was enlightened once for all upon women's logic by the Matrimonial Gadfly, "you are right: but then you know the baby is in splendid health, here."

Though Adolphe has become prudent, this reply awakens Caroline's susceptibilities. A mother is very willing to think exclusively of her child, but she does not want him to be preferred to herself. She is silent; the next day, she is tired to death of the country. Adolphe being absent on business, she waits for him from five o'clock to seven, and goes alone with little Charles to the coach office. She talks for three-quarters of an hour of her anxieties. She was afraid to go from the house to the office. Is it proper for a young woman to be left alone, so? She cannot support such an existence.

The country house now creates a very peculiar phase; one which deserves a chapter to itself.

TROUBLE WITHIN TROUBLE.

Axiom.—There are parentheses in worry.

EXAMPLE—A great deal of evil has been said of the stitch in the side; but it is nothing to the stitch to which we now refer, which the pleasures of the matrimonial second crop are everlastingly reviving, like the hammer of a note in the piano. This constitutes an irritant, which never flourishes except at the period when the young wife's timidity gives place to that fatal equality of rights which is at once devastating France and the conjugal relation. Every season has its peculiar vexation.

Caroline, after a week spent in taking note of her husband's absences, perceives that he passes seven hours a day away from her. At last, Adolphe, who comes home as gay as an actor who has been applauded, observes a slight coating of hoar frost upon Caroline's visage. After making sure that the coldness of her manner has been observed, Caroline puts on a counterfeit air of interest,—the well-known expression of which possesses the gift of making a man inwardly swear,—and says: "You must have had a good deal of business to-day, dear?"

"Oh, lots!"

"Did you take many cabs?"

"I took seven francs' worth."

"Did you find everybody in?"

"Yes, those with whom I had appointments."

"When did you make appointments with them? The ink in your inkstand is dried up; it's like glue; I wanted to write, and spent a whole hour in moistening it, and even then only produced a thick mud fit to mark bundles with for the East Indies."

Here any and every husband looks suspiciously at his better half.

"It is probable that I wrote them at Paris—"

"What business was it, Adolphe?"

"Why, I thought you knew. Shall I run over the list? First, there's Chaumontel's affair—"

"I thought Monsieur Chaumontel was in Switzerland—"

"Yes, but he has representatives, a lawyer—"

"Didn't you do anything else but business?" asks Caroline, interrupting Adolphe.

Here she gives him a direct, piercing look, by which she plunges into her husband's eyes when he least expects it: a sword in a heart.

"What could I have done? Made a little counterfeit money, run into debt, or embroidered a sampler?"

"Oh, dear, I don't know. And I can't even guess. I am too dull, you've told me so a hundred times."

"There you go, and take an expression of endearment in bad part. How like a woman that is!"

"Have you concluded anything?" she asks, pretending to take an interest in business.

"No, nothing,"

"How many persons have you seen?"

"Eleven, without counting those who were walking in the streets."

"How you answer me!"

"Yes, and how you question me! As if you'd been following the trade of an examining judge for the last ten years!"

"Come, tell me all you've done to-day, it will amuse me. You ought to try to please me while you are here! I'm dull enough when you leave me alone all day long."

"You want me to amuse you by telling you about business?"

64

"Formerly, you told me everything—"

This friendly little reproach disguises the certitude that Caroline wishes to enjoy respecting the serious matters which Adolphe wishes to conceal. Adolphe then undertakes to narrate how he has spent the day. Caroline affects a sort of distraction sufficiently well played to induce the belief that she is not listening.

"But you said just now," she exclaims, at the moment when Adolphe is getting into a snarl, "that you had paid seven francs for cabs, and you now talk of a hack! You took it by the hour, I suppose? Did you do your business in a hack?" she asks, railingly.

"Why should hacks be interdicted?" inquires Adolphe, resuming his narrative.

"Haven't you been to Madame de Fischtaminel's?" she asks in the middle of an exceedingly involved explanation, insolently taking the words out of your mouth.

"Why should I have been there?"

"It would have given me pleasure: I wanted to know whether her parlor is done."

"It is."

"Ah! then you *have* been there?"

"No, her upholsterer told me."

"Do you know her upholsterer?"

"Yes."

"Who is it?"

"Braschon."

"So you met the upholsterer?"

"Yes."

"You said you only went in carriages."

"Yes, my dear, but to get carriages, you have to go and—"

"Pooh! I dare say Braschon was in the carriage, or the parlor was—one or the other is equally probable."

"You won't listen," exclaims Adolphe, who thinks that a long story will lull Caroline's suspicions.

"I've listened too much already. You've been lying for the last hour, worse than a drummer."

"Well, I'll say nothing more."

"I know enough. I know all I wanted to know. You say you've seen lawyers, notaries, bankers: now you haven't seen one of them! Suppose I were to go to-morrow to see Madame de Fischtaminel, do you know what she would say?"

Here, Caroline watches Adolphe closely: but Adolphe affects a delusive calmness, in the middle of which Caroline throws out her line to fish up a clue.

"Why, she would say that she had had the pleasure of seeing you! How wretched we poor creatures are! We never know what you are doing: here we are stuck, chained at home, while you are off at your business! Fine business, truly! If I were in your place, I would invent business a little bit better put together than yours! Ah, you set us a worthy example! They say women are perverse. Who perverted them?"

Here Adolphe tries, by looking fixedly at Caroline, to arrest the torrent of words. Caroline, like a horse who has just been touched up by the lash, starts off anew, and with the animation of one of Rossini's codas:

"Yes, it's a very neat idea, to put your wife out in the country so that you may spend the day as you like at Paris. So this is the cause of your passion for a country house! Snipe that I was, to be caught in the trap! You are right, sir, a villa is very convenient: it serves two objects. But the wife can get along with it as well as the husband. You may take Paris and its hacks! I'll take the woods and their shady groves! Yes, Adolphe, I am really satisfied, so let's say no more about it."

Adolphe listens to sarcasm for an hour by the clock.

"Have you done, dear?" he asks, profiting by an instant in which she tosses her head after a pointed interrogation.

Then Caroline concludes thus: "I've had enough of the villa, and I'll never set foot in it again. But I know what will happen: you'll keep it, probably, and leave me in Paris. Well, at Paris, I can at least amuse myself, while you go with Madame de Fischtaminel to the woods. What is a *Villa Adolphini* where you get nauseated if you go six times round the lawn? where they've planted chair-legs and broom-sticks on the pretext of producing shade? It's like a furnace: the walls are six inches thick! and my gentleman is absent seven hours a day! That's what a country seat means!"

"Listen to me, Caroline."

"I wouldn't so much mind, if you would only confess what you did to-day. You don't know me yet: come, tell me, I won't scold you. I pardon you beforehand for all that you've done."

Adolphe, who knows the consequences of a confession too well to make one to his wife, replies—"Well, I'll tell you."

"That's a good fellow—I shall love you better."

"I was three hours—"

"I was sure of it—at Madame de Fischtaminel's!"

"No, at our notary's, as he had got me a purchaser; but we could not come to terms: he wanted our villa furnished. When I left there, I went to Braschon's, to see how much we owed him—"

"You made up this romance while I was talking to you! Look me in the face! I'll go to see Braschon to-morrow."

Adolphe cannot restrain a nervous shudder.

"You can't help laughing, you monster!"

"I laugh at your obstinacy."

"I'll go to-morrow to Madame de Fischtaminel's."

"Oh, go wherever you like!"

"What brutality!" says Caroline, rising and going away with her handkerchief at her eyes.

The country house, so ardently longed for by Caroline, has now become a diabolical invention of Adolphe's, a trap into which the fawn has fallen.

Since Adolphe's discovery that it is impossible to reason with Caroline, he lets her say whatever she pleases.

Two months after, he sells the villa which cost him twenty-two thousand francs for seven thousand! But he gains this by the adventure—he finds out that the country is not the thing that Caroline wants.

The question is becoming serious. Nature, with its woods, its forests, its valleys, the Switzerland of the environs of Paris, the artificial rivers, have amused Caroline for barely six months. Adolphe is tempted to abdicate and take Caroline's part himself.

A HOUSEHOLD REVOLUTION.

One morning, Adolphe is seized by the triumphant idea of letting Caroline find out for herself what she wants. He gives up to her the control of the house, saying, "Do as you like." He substitutes the constitutional system for the autocratic system, a responsible ministry for an absolute conjugal monarchy. This proof of confidence —the object of much secret envy—is, to women, a field-marshal's baton. Women are then, so to speak, mistresses at home.

After this, nothing, not even the memory of the honey-moon, can be compared to Adolphe's happiness for several days. A woman, under such circumstances, is all sugar. She is too sweet: she would invent the art of petting and cosseting and of coining tender little names, if this matrimonial sugar-plummery had not existed ever since the Terrestrial Paradise. At the end of the month, Adolphe's condition is like that of children towards the close of New Year's week. So Caroline is beginning to say, not in words, but in acts, in manner, in mimetic expressions: "It's difficult to tell *what* to do to please a man!"

Giving up the helm of the boat to one's wife, is an exceedingly ordinary idea, and would hardly deserve the qualification of "triumphant," which we have given it at the commencement of this chapter, if it were not accompanied by that of taking it back again. Adolphe was seduced by a wish, which invariably seizes persons who are the prey of misfortune, to know how far an evil will go!—to try how much damage fire will do when left to itself, the individual possessing, or thinking he possesses, the power to arrest it. This curiosity pursues us from the cradle to the grave. Then, after his plethora of conjugal felicity, Adolphe, who is treating himself to a farce in his own house, goes through the following phases:

FIRST EPOCH. Things go on altogether too well. Caroline buys little account books to keep a list of her expenses in, she buys a nice little piece of furniture to store her money in, she feeds Adolphe superbly, she is happy in his approbation, she discovers that very many articles are needed in the house. It is her ambition to be an incomparable housekeeper. Adolphe, who arrogates to himself the right of censorship, no longer finds the slightest suggestion to make.

When he dresses himself, everything is ready to his hands. Not even in Armide's garden was more ingenious tenderness displayed than that of Caroline. For her phoenix husband, she renews the wax upon his razor strap, she substitutes new suspenders for old ones. None of his button-holes are ever widowed. His linen is as well cared for as that of the confessor of the devotee, all whose sins are venial. His stockings are free from holes. At table, his tastes, his caprices even, are studied, consulted: he is getting fat! There is ink in his inkstand, and the sponge is always moist. He never has occasion to say, like Louis XIV, "I came near having to wait!" In short, he hears himself continually called *a love of a man*. He is obliged to reproach Caroline for neglecting herself: she does not pay sufficient attention to her own needs. Of this gentle reproach Caroline takes note.

SECOND EPOCH. The scene changes, at table. Everything is exceedingly dear. Vegetables are beyond one's means. Wood sells as if it came from Campeche. Fruit? Oh! as to fruit, princes, bankers and great lords alone can eat it. Dessert is a cause of ruin. Adolphe often hears Caroline say to Madame Deschars: "How do you manage?" Conferences are held in your presence upon the proper way to keep cooks under the thumb.

A cook who entered your service without effects, without clothes, and without talent, has come to get her wages in a blue merino gown, set off by an embroidered neckerchief, her ears embellished with a pair of ear-rings enriched with small pearls, her feet clothed in comfortable shoes which give you a glimpse of neat cotton stockings. She has two trunks full of property, and keeps an account at the savings bank.

Upon this Caroline complains of the bad morals of the lower classes: she complains of the education and the knowledge of figures which distinguish domestics. From time to time she utters little axioms like the following: There are some mistakes you *must* make!—It's only those who do nothing who do everything well.—She has the anxieties that belong to power.—Ah! men are fortunate in not having a house to keep.—Women bear the burden of the innumerable details.

THIRD EPOCH. Caroline, absorbed in the idea that you should eat merely to live, treats Adolphe to the delights of a cenobitic table.

Adolphe's stockings are either full of holes or else rough with the lichen of hasty mendings, for the day is not long enough for all that his wife has to do. He wears suspenders blackened by use. His linen is old and gapes like a door-keeper, or like the door itself. At a time when Adolphe is in haste to conclude a matter of business, it takes him an hour to dress: he has to pick out his garments one by one, opening many an article before finding one fit to wear. But Caroline is charmingly dressed. She has pretty bonnets, velvet boots, mantillas. She has made up her mind, she conducts her administration in virtue of this principle: Charity well understood begins at home. When Adolphe complains of the contrast between his poverty-stricken wardrobe and Caroline's splendor, she says, "Why, you reproached me with buying nothing for myself!"

The husband and the wife here begin to bandy jests more or less acrimonious. One evening Caroline makes herself very agreeable, in order to insinuate an avowal of a rather large deficit, just as the ministry begins to eulogize the tax-payers, and boast of the wealth of the country, when it is preparing to bring forth a bill for an additional appropriation. There is this further similitude that both are done in the chamber, whether in administration or in housekeeping. From this springs the profound truth that the constitutional system is infinitely dearer than the monarchical system. For a nation as for a household, it is the government of the happy balance, of mediocrity, of chicanery.

Adolphe, enlightened by his past annoyances, waits for an opportunity to explode, and Caroline slumbers in a delusive security.

What starts the quarrel? Do we ever know what electric current precipitates the avalanche or decides a revolution? It may result from anything or nothing. But finally, Adolphe, after a period to be determined in each case by the circumstances of the couple, utters this fatal phrase, in the midst of a discussion: "Ah! when I was a bachelor!"

Her husband's bachelor life is to a woman what the phrase, "My dear deceased," is to a widow's second husband. These two stings produce wounds which are never completely healed.

Then Adolphe goes on like General Bonaparte haranguing the Five Hundred: "We are on a volcano!—The house no longer has a head, the time to come to an understanding has arrived.—You talk of happiness, Caroline, but you have compromised, imperiled it by your exactions, you have violated the civil code: you have mixed yourself up in the discussions of business, and you have invaded the conjugal authority. —We must reform our internal affairs."

Caroline does not shout, like the Five Hundred, "Down with the dictator!" For people never shout a man down, when they feel that they can put him down.

"When I was a bachelor I had none but new stockings! I had a clean napkin every day on my plate. The restaurateur only fleeced me of a determinate sum. I have given up to you my beloved liberty! What have you done with it?"

"Am I then so very wrong, Adolphe, to have sought to spare you numerous cares?" says Caroline, taking an attitude before her husband. "Take the key of the money-box back,—but do you know what will happen? I am ashamed, but you will compel me to go on to the stage to get the merest necessaries of life. Is this what you want? Degrade your wife, or bring in conflict two contrary, hostile interests—"

Such, for three quarters of the French people is an exact definition of marriage.

"Be perfectly easy, dear," resumes Caroline, seating herself in her chair like Marius on the ruins of Carthage, "I will never ask you for anything. I am not a beggar! I know what I'll do—you don't know me yet."

"Well, what will you do?" asks Adolphe; "it seems impossible to joke or have an explanation with you women. What will you do?"

"It doesn't concern you at all."

"Excuse me, madame, quite the contrary. Dignity, honor—"

"Oh, have no fear of that, sir. For your sake more than for my own, I will keep it a dead secret."

"Come, Caroline, my own Carola, what do you mean to do?"

Caroline darts a viper-like glance at Adolphe, who recoils and proceeds to walk up and down the room.

"There now, tell me, what will you do?" he repeats after much too prolonged a silence.

"I shall go to work, sir!"

At this sublime declaration, Adolphe executes a movement in retreat, detecting a bitter exasperation, and feeling the sharpness of a north wind which had never before blown in the matrimonial chamber.

THE ART OF BEING A VICTIM.

On and after the Revolution, our vanquished Caroline adopts an infernal system, the effect of which is to make you regret your victory every hour. She becomes the opposition! Should Adolphe have one more such triumph, he would appear before the Court of Assizes, accused of having smothered his wife between two mattresses, like Shakespeare's Othello. Caroline puts on the air of a martyr; her submission is positively killing. On every occasion she assassinates Adolphe with a "Just as you like!" uttered in tones whose sweetness is something fearful. No elegiac poet could compete with Caroline, who utters elegy upon elegy: elegy in action, elegy in speech: her smile is elegiac, her silence is elegiac, her gestures are elegiac. Here are a few examples, wherein every household will find some of its impressions recorded:

AFTER BREAKFAST. "Caroline, we go to-night to the Deschars' grand ball you know."

"Yes, love."

AFTER DINNER. "What, not dressed yet, Caroline?" exclaims Adolphe, who has just made his appearance, magnificently equipped.

He finds Caroline arrayed in a gown fit for an elderly lady of strong conversational powers, a black moire with an old-fashioned fan-waist. Flowers, too badly imitated to deserve the name of artificial, give a gloomy aspect to a head of hair which the chambermaid has carelessly arranged. Caroline's gloves have already seen wear and tear.

"I am ready, my dear."

"What, in that dress?"

"I have no other. A new dress would have cost three hundred francs."

"Why did you not tell me?"

"I, ask you for anything, after what has happened!"

"I'll go alone," says Adolphe, unwilling to be humiliated in his wife.

"I dare say you are very glad to," returns Caroline, in a captious tone, "it's plain enough from the way you are got up."

Eleven persons are in the parlor, all invited to dinner by Adolphe. Caroline is there, looking as if her husband had invited her too. She is waiting for dinner to be served.

"Sir," says the parlor servant in a whisper to his master, "the cook doesn't know what on earth to do!"

"What's the matter?"

"You said nothing to her, sir: and she has only two side-dishes, the beef, a chicken, a salad and vegetables."

"Caroline, didn't you give the necessary orders?"

"How did I know that you had company, and besides I can't take it upon myself to give orders here! You delivered me from all care on that point, and I thank heaven for it every day of my life."

Madame de Fischtaminel has called to pay Madame Caroline a visit. She finds her coughing feebly and nearly bent double over her embroidery.

"Ah, so you are working those slippers for your dear Adolphe?"

Adolphe is standing before the fire-place as complacently as may be.

"No, madame, it's for a tradesman who pays me for them: like the convicts, my labor enables me to treat myself to some little comforts."

Adolphe reddens; he can't very well beat his wife, and Madame de Fischtaminel looks at him as much as to say, "What does this mean?"

"You cough a good deal, my darling," says Madame de Fischtaminel.

"Oh!" returns Caroline, "what is life to me?"

Caroline is seated, conversing with a lady of your acquaintance, whose good opinion you are exceedingly anxious to retain. From the depths of the embrasure where you are talking with some friends, you gather, from the mere motion of her lips, these words: "My husband would have it so!" uttered with the air of a young Roman matron going to the circus to be devoured. You are profoundly wounded in your several vanities, and wish to attend to this conversation while listening to your guests: you thus make replies which bring you back such inquiries as: "Why, what are you thinking of?" For you have lost the thread of the discourse, and you fidget nervously with your feet, thinking to yourself, "What is she telling her about me?"

Adolphe is dining with the Deschars: twelve persons are at table, and Caroline is seated next to a nice young man named Ferdinand, Adolphe's cousin. Between the first and second course, conjugal happiness is the subject of conversation.

"There is nothing easier than for a woman to be happy," says Caroline in reply to a woman who complains of her husband.

"Tell us your secret, madame," says M. de Fischtaminel agreeably.

"A woman has nothing to do but to meddle with nothing to consider herself as the first servant in the house or as a slave that the master takes care of, to have no will of her own, and never to make an observation: thus all goes well."

This, delivered in a bitter tone and with tears in her voice, alarms Adolphe, who looks fixedly at his wife.

"You forget, madame, the happiness of telling about one's happiness," he returns, darting at her a glance worthy of the tyrant in a melodrama.

Quite satisfied with having shown herself assassinated or on the point of being so, Caroline turns her head aside, furtively wipes away a tear, and says:

"Happiness cannot be described!"

This incident, as they say at the Chamber, leads to nothing, but Ferdinand looks upon his cousin as an angel about to be offered up.

Some one alludes to the frightful prevalence of inflammation of the stomach, or to the nameless diseases of which young women die.

"Ah, too happy they!" exclaims Caroline, as if she were foretelling the manner of her death.

Adolphe's mother-in-law comes to see her daughter. Caroline says, "My husband's parlor:" "Your master's chamber." Everything in the house belongs to "My husband."

"Why, what's the matter, children?" asks the mother-in-law; "you seem to be at swords' points."

"Oh, dear me," says Adolphe, "nothing but that Caroline has had the management of the house and didn't manage it right, that's all."

"She got into debt, I suppose?"

"Yes, dearest mamma."

"Look here, Adolphe," says the mother-in-law, after having waited to be left alone with her son, "would you prefer to have my daughter magnificently dressed, to have everything go on smoothly, *without its costing you anything*?"

Imagine, if you can, the expression of Adolphe's physiognomy, as he hears *this declaration of woman's rights*!

Caroline abandons her shabby dress and appears in a splendid one. She is at the Deschars': every one compliments her upon her taste, upon the richness of her materials, upon her lace, her jewels.

"Ah! you have a charming husband!" says Madame Deschars. Adolphe tosses his head proudly, and looks at Caroline.

"My husband, madame! I cost that gentleman nothing, thank heaven! All I have was given me by my mother."

Adolphe turns suddenly about and goes to talk with Madame de Fischtaminel.

After a year of absolute monarchy, Caroline says very mildly one morning:

"How much have you spent this year, dear?"

"I don't know."

"Examine your accounts."

Adolphe discovers that he has spent a third more than during Caroline's worst year.

"And I've cost you nothing for my dress," she adds.

Caroline is playing Schubert's melodies. Adolphe takes great pleasure in hearing these compositions well-executed: he gets up and compliments Caroline. She bursts into tears.

"What's the matter?"

"Nothing, I'm nervous."

"I didn't know you were subject to that."

"O Adolphe, you won't see anything! Look, my rings come off my fingers: you don't love me any more—I'm a burden to you—"

She weeps, she won't listen, she weeps afresh at every word Adolphe utters.

"Suppose you take the management of the house back again?"

"Ah!" she exclaims, rising sharply to her feet, like a spring figure in a box, "now that you've had enough of your experience! Thank you! Do you suppose it's money that I want? Singular method, yours, of pouring balm upon a wounded heart. No, go away."

"Very well, just as you like, Caroline."

This "just as you like" is the first expression of indifference towards a wife: and Caroline sees before her an abyss towards which she had been walking of her own free will.

THE FRENCH CAMPAIGN.

The disasters of 1814 afflict every species of existence. After brilliant days of conquest, after the period during which obstacles change to triumphs, and the slightest check becomes a piece of good fortune, there comes a time when the happiest ideas turn out blunders, when courage leads to destruction, and when your very fortifications are a stumbling-block. Conjugal love, which, according to authors, is a peculiar phase of love, has, more than anything else, its French Campaign, its fatal 1814. The devil especially loves to dangle his tail in the affairs of poor desolate women, and to this Caroline has come.

Caroline is trying to think of some means of bringing her husband back. She spends many solitary hours at home, and during this time her imagination works. She goes and comes, she gets up, and often stands pensively at the window, looking at the street and seeing nothing, her face glued to the panes, and feeling as if in a desert, in the midst of her friends, in the bosom of her luxuriously furnished apartments.

Now, in Paris, unless a person occupy a house of his own, enclosed between a court and a garden, all life is double. At every story, a family sees another family in the opposite house. Everybody plunges his gaze at will into his neighbor's domains. There is a necessity for mutual observation, a common right of search from which none can escape. At a given time, in the morning, you get up early, the servant opposite is dusting the parlor, she has left the windows open and has put the rugs on the railing; you divine a multitude of things, and vice-versa. Thus, in a given time, you are acquainted with the habits of the pretty, the old, the young, the coquettish, the virtuous woman opposite, or the caprices of the coxcomb, the inventions of the old bachelor, the color of the furniture, and the cat of the two pair front. Everything furnishes a hint, and becomes matter for divination. At the fourth story, a grisette, taken by surprise, finds herself—too late, like the chaste Susanne,—the prey of the delighted lorgnette of an aged clerk, who earns eighteen hundred francs a year, and who becomes criminal gratis. On the other hand, a handsome young gentleman, who, for the present, works without wages, and is only nineteen years old, appears before the sight of a pious old lady, in the simple apparel of a man engaged in shaving. The watch thus kept up is never relaxed, while prudence, on the contrary, has its moments of forgetfulness. Curtains are not always let down in time. A woman, just before dark, approaches the window to thread her needle, and the married man opposite may then admire a head that Raphael might have painted, and one that he considers worthy of himself—a National Guard truly imposing when under arms. Oh, sacred private life, where art thou! Paris is a city ever ready to exhibit itself half naked, a city essentially libertine and devoid of modesty. For a person's life to be decorous in it, the said person should have a hundred thousand a year. Virtues are dearer than vices in Paris.

Caroline, whose gaze sometimes steals between the protecting muslins which hide her domestic life from the five stories opposite, at last discovers a young couple plunged in the delights of the honey-moon, and newly established in the first story directly in view of her window. She spends her time in the most exciting observations. The blinds are closed early, and opened late. One day, Caroline, who has arisen at eight o'clock notices, by accident, of course, the maid preparing a bath or a morning dress, a delicious deshabille. Caroline sighs. She lies in ambush like a hunter at the cover; she surprises the young woman, her face actually illuminated with happiness. Finally, by dint of watching the charming couple, she sees the gentleman and lady open the window, and lean gently one against the other, as, supported by the railing, they breathe the evening air. Caroline gives herself a nervous headache, by endeavoring to interpret the phantasmagorias, some of them having an explanation and others not, made by the shadows of these two young people on the curtains, one night when they have forgotten to close the shutters. The young woman is often seated, melancholy and pensive, waiting for her absent husband; she hears the tread of a horse, or the rumble of a cab at the street corner; she starts from the sofa, and from her movements, it is easy for Caroline to see that she exclaims: "'Tis he!"

"How they love each other!" says Caroline to herself.

By dint of nervous headache, Caroline conceives an exceedingly ingenious plan: this plan consists in using the conjugal bliss of the opposite neighbors as a tonic to stimulate Adolphe. The idea is not without depravity, but then Caroline's intention sanctifies the means!

"Adolphe," she says, "we have a neighbor opposite, the loveliest woman, a brunette—"

"Oh, yes," returns Adolphe, "I know her. She is a friend of Madame de Fischtaminel's: Madame Foullepointe, the wife of a broker, a charming man and a good fellow, very fond of his wife: he's crazy about her. His office and rooms are here, in the court, while those on the street are madame's. I know of no happier household. Foullepointe talks about his happiness everywhere, even at the Exchange; he's really quite tiresome."

"Well, then, be good enough to present Monsieur and Madame Foullepointe to me. I should be delighted to learn how she manages to make her husband love her so much: have they been married long?"

"Five years, just like us."

"O Adolphe, dear, I am dying to know her: make us intimately acquainted. Am I as pretty as she?"

"Well, if I were to meet you at an opera ball, and if you weren't my wife, I declare, I shouldn't know which—"

"You are real sweet to-day. Don't forget to invite them to dinner Saturday."

"I'll do it to-night. Foullepointe and I often meet on 'Change."

"Now," says Caroline, "this young woman will doubtless tell me what her method of action is."

Caroline resumes her post of observation. At about three she looks through the flowers which form as it were a bower at the window, and exclaims, "Two perfect doves!"

For the Saturday in question, Caroline invites Monsieur and Madame Deschars, the worthy Monsieur Fischtaminel, in short, the most virtuous couples of her society. She has brought out all her resources: she has ordered the most sumptuous dinner, she has taken the silver out of the chest: she means to do all honor to the model of wives.

"My dear, you will see to-night," she says to Madame Deschars, at the moment when all the women are looking at each other in silence, "the most admirable young couple in the world, our opposite neighbors: a young man of fair complexion, so graceful and with *such* manners! His head is like Lord Byron's, and he's a real Don Juan, only faithful: he's discovered the secret of making love eternal: I shall perhaps obtain a second crop of it from her example. Adolphe, when he sees them, will blush at his conduct, and—"

The servant announces: "Monsieur and Madame Foullepointe."

Madame Foullepointe, a pretty brunette, a genuine Parisian, slight and erect in form, the brilliant light of her eye quenched by her long lashes, charmingly dressed, sits down upon the sofa. Caroline bows to a fat gentleman with thin gray hair, who follows this Paris Andalusian, and who exhibits a face and paunch fit for Silenus, a butter-colored pate, a deceitful, libertine smile upon his big, heavy lips,—in short, a philosopher! Caroline looks upon this individual with astonishment.

"Monsieur Foullepointe, my dear," says Adolphe, presenting the worthy quinquagenarian.

"I am delighted, madame," says Caroline, good-naturedly, "that you have brought your father-in-law [profound sensation], but we shall soon see your husband, I trust—"

"Madame—!"

Everybody listens and looks. Adolphe becomes the object of every one's attention; he is literally dumb with amazement: if he could, he would whisk Caroline off through a trap, as at the theatre.

"This is Monsieur Foullepointe, my husband," says Madame Foullepointe.

Caroline turns scarlet as she sees her ridiculous blunder, and Adolphe scathes her with a look of thirty-six candlepower.

"You said he was young and fair," whispers Madame Deschars. Madame Foullepointe,—knowing lady that she is,—boldly stares at the ceiling.

A month after, Madame Foullepointe and Caroline become intimate. Adolphe, who is taken up with Madame de Fischtaminel, pays no attention to this dangerous friendship, a friendship which will bear its fruits, for—pray learn this—

Axiom.—Women have corrupted more women than men have ever loved.

A SOLO ON THE HEARSE.

After a period, the length of which depends on the strength of Caroline's principles, she appears to be languishing; and when Adolphe, anxious for decorum's sake, as he sees her stretched out upon the sofa like a snake in the sun, asks her, "What is the matter, love? What do you want?"

"I wish I was dead!" she replies.

"Quite a merry and agreeable wish!"

"It isn't death that frightens me, it's suffering."

"I suppose that means that I don't make you happy! That's the way with women!"

Adolphe strides about the room, talking incoherently: but he is brought to a dead halt by seeing Caroline dry her tears, which are really flowing artistically, in an embroidered handkerchief.

"Do you feel sick?"

"I don't feel well. [Silence.] I only hope that I shall live long enough to see my daughter married, for I know the meaning, now, of the expression so little understood by the young—*the choice of a husband*! Go to your amusements, Adolphe: a woman who thinks of the future, a woman who suffers, is not at all diverting: come, go and have a good time."

"Where do you feel bad?"

"I don't feel bad, dear: I never was better. I don't feel anything. No, really, I am better. There, leave me to myself."

This time, being the first, Adolphe goes away almost sad.

A week passes, during which Caroline orders all the servants to conceal from her husband her deplorable situation: she languishes, she rings when she feels she is going off, she uses a great deal of ether. The domestics finally acquaint their master with madame's conjugal heroism, and Adolphe remains at home one evening after dinner, and sees his wife passionately kissing her little Marie.

"Poor child! I regret the future only for your sake! What is life, I should like to know?"

"Come, my dear," says Adolphe, "don't take on so."

"I'm not taking on. Death doesn't frighten me—I saw a funeral this morning, and I thought how happy the body was! How comes it that I think of nothing but death? Is it a disease? I have an idea that I shall die by my own hand."

The more Adolphe tries to divert Caroline, the more closely she wraps herself up in the crape of her hopeless melancholy. This second time, Adolphe stays at home and is wearied to death. At the third attack of forced tears, he goes out without the slightest compunction. He finally gets accustomed to these everlasting murmurs, to these dying postures, these crocodile tears. So he says:

"If you are sick, Caroline, you'd better have a doctor."

"Just as you like! It will end quicker, so. But bring a famous one, if you bring any."

At the end of a month, Adolphe, worn out by hearing the funereal air that Caroline plays him on every possible key, brings home a famous doctor. At Paris, doctors are all men of discernment, and are admirably versed in conjugal nosography.

"Well, madame," says the great physician, "how happens it that so pretty a woman allows herself to be sick?"

"Ah! sir, like the nose of old father Aubry, I aspire to the tomb—"

Caroline, out of consideration for Adolphe, makes a feeble effort to smile.

"Tut, tut! But your eyes are clear: they don't seem to need our infernal drugs."

"Look again, doctor, I am eaten up with fever, a slow, imperceptible fever—"

And she fastens her most roguish glance upon the illustrious doctor, who says to himself, "What eyes!"

"Now, let me see your tongue."

Caroline puts out her taper tongue between two rows of teeth as white as those of a dog.

"It is a little bit furred at the root: but you have breakfasted—" observes the great physician, turning toward Adolphe.

"Oh, a mere nothing," returns Caroline; "two cups of tea—"

Adolphe and the illustrious leech look at each other, for the doctor wonders whether it is the husband or the wife that is trifling with him.

"What do you feel?" gravely inquires the physician.

"I don't sleep."

"Good!"

"I have no appetite."

"Well!"

"I have a pain, here."

The doctor examines the part indicated.

"Very good, we'll look at that by and by."

"Now and then a shudder passes over me—"

"Very good!"

"I have melancholy fits, I am always thinking of death, I feel promptings of suicide—"

"Dear me! Really!"

"I have rushes of heat to the face: look, there's a constant trembling in my eyelid."

"Capital! We call that a trismus."

The doctor goes into an explanation, which lasts a quarter of an hour, of the trismus, employing the most scientific terms. From this it appears that the trismus is the trismus: but he observes with the greatest modesty that if science knows that the trismus is the trismus, it is entirely ignorant of the cause of this nervous affection, which comes and goes, appears and disappears—"and," he adds, "we have decided that it is altogether nervous."

"Is it very dangerous?" asks Caroline, anxiously.

"Not at all. How do you lie at night?"

"Doubled up in a heap."

"Good. On which side?"

"The left."

"Very well. How many mattresses are there on your bed?"

"Three."

"Good. Is there a spring bed?"

"Yes."

"What is the spring bed stuffed with?"

"Horse hair."

"Capital. Let me see you walk. No, no, naturally, and as if we weren't looking at you."

Caroline walks like Fanny Elssler, communicating the most Andalusian little motions to her tournure.

"Do you feel a sensation of heaviness in your knees?"

"Well, no—" she returns to her place. "Ah, no that I think of it, it seems to me that I do."

"Good. Have you been in the house a good deal lately?"

"Oh, yes, sir, a great deal too much—and alone."

"Good. I thought so. What do you wear on your head at night?"

"An embroidered night-cap, and sometimes a handkerchief over it."

"Don't you feel a heat there, a slight perspiration?"

"How can I, when I'm asleep?"

"Don't you find your night-cap moist on your forehead, when you wake up?"

"Sometimes."

"Capital. Give me your hand."

The doctor takes out his watch.

"Did I tell you that I have a vertigo?" asks Caroline.

"Hush!" says the doctor, counting the pulse. "In the evening?"

"No, in the morning."

"Ah, bless me, a vertigo in the morning," says the doctor, looking at Adolphe.

"The Duke of G. has not gone to London," says the great physician, while examining Caroline's skin, "and there's a good deal to be said about it in the Faubourg St. Germain."

"Have you patients there?" asks Caroline.

"Nearly all my patients are there. Dear me, yes; I've got seven to see this morning; some of them are in danger."

"What do you think of me, sir?" says Caroline.

"Madame, you need attention, a great deal of attention, you must take quieting liquors, plenty of syrup of gum, a mild diet, white meat, and a good deal of exercise."

"There go twenty francs," says Adolphe to himself with a smile.

The great physician takes Adolphe by the arm, and draws him out with him, as he takes his leave: Caroline follows them on tiptoe.

"My dear sir," says the great physician, "I have just prescribed very insufficiently for your wife. I did not wish to frighten her: this affair concerns you more nearly than you imagine. Don't neglect her; she has a powerful temperament, and enjoys violent health; all this reacts upon her. Nature has its laws, which, when disregarded, compel obedience. She may get into a morbid state, which would cause you bitterly to repent having neglected her. If you love her, why, love her: but if you don't love her, and nevertheless desire to preserve the mother of your children, the resolution to come to is a matter of hygiene, but it can only proceed from you!"

"How well he understand me!" says Caroline to herself. She opens the door and says: "Doctor, you did not write down the doses!"

The great physician smiles, bows and slips the twenty franc piece into his pocket; he then leaves Adolphe to his wife, who takes him and says:

"What is the fact about my condition? Must I prepare for death?"

"Bah! He says you're too healthy!" cries Adolphe, impatiently.

Caroline retires to her sofa to weep.

"What is it, now?"

"So I am to live a long time—I am in the way—you don't love me any more—I won't consult that doctor again—I don't know why Madame Foullepointe advised me to see him, he told me nothing but trash—I know better than he what I need!"

"What do you need?"

"Can you ask, ungrateful man?" and Caroline leans her head on Adolphe's shoulder.

Adolphe, very much alarmed, says to himself: "The doctor's right, she may get to be morbidly exacting, and then what will become of me? Here I am compelled to choose between Caroline's physical extravagance, or some young cousin or other."

Meanwhile Caroline sits down and sings one of Schubert's melodies with all the agitation of a hypochondriac.

PART SECOND

PREFACE

If, reader, you have grasped the intent of this book,—and infinite honor is done you by the supposition: the profoundest author does not always comprehend, I may say never comprehends, the different meanings of his book, nor its bearing, nor the good nor the harm it may do—if, then, you have bestowed some attention upon these little scenes of married life, you have perhaps noticed their color—

"What color?" some grocer will doubtless ask; "books are bound in yellow, blue, green, pearl-gray, white—"

Alas! books possess another color, they are dyed by the author, and certain writers borrow their dye. Some books let their color come off on to others. More than this. Books are dark or fair, light brown or red. They have a sex, too! I know of male books, and female books, of books which, sad to say, have no sex, which we hope is not the case with this one, supposing that you do this collection of nosographic sketches the honor of calling it a book.

Thus far, the troubles we have described have been exclusively inflicted by the wife upon the husband. You have therefore seen only the masculine side of the book. And if the author really has the sense of hearing for which we give him credit, he has already caught more than one indignant exclamation or remonstrance:

"He tells us of nothing but vexations suffered by our husbands, as if we didn't have our petty troubles, too!"

Oh, women! You have been heard, for if you do not always make yourselves understood, you are always sure to make yourselves heard.

It would therefore be signally unjust to lay upon you alone the reproaches that every being brought under the yoke (*conjugium*) has the right to heap upon that necessary, sacred, useful, eminently conservative institution,—one, however, that is often somewhat of an encumbrance, and tight about the joints, though sometimes it is also too loose there.

I will go further! Such partiality would be a piece of idiocy.

A man,—not a writer, for in a writer there are many men,—an author, rather, should resemble Janus, see behind and before, become a spy, examine an idea in all its phases, delve alternately into the soul of Alceste and into that of Philaenete, know everything though he does not tell it, never be tiresome, and—

We will not conclude this programme, for we should tell the whole, and that would be frightful for those who reflect upon the present condition of literature.

Furthermore, an author who speaks for himself in the middle of his book, resembles the old fellow in "The Speaking Picture," when he puts his face in the hole cut in the painting. The author does not forget that in the Chamber, no one can take the floor *between two votes*. Enough, therefore!

Here follows the female portion of the book: for, to resemble marriage perfectly, it ought to be more or less hermaphroditic.

HUSBANDS DURING THE SECOND MONTH.

Two young married women, Caroline and Stephanie, who had been early friends at M'lle Machefer's boarding school, one of the most celebrated educational institutions in the Faubourg St. Honore, met at a ball given by Madame de Fischtaminel, and the following conversation took place in a window-seat in the boudoir.

It was so hot that a man had acted upon the idea of going to breathe the fresh night air, some time before the two young women. He had placed himself in the angle of the balcony, and, as there were many flowers before the window, the two friends thought themselves alone. This man was the author's best friend.

One of the two ladies, standing at the corner of the embrasure, kept watch by looking at the boudoir and the parlors. The other had so placed herself as not to be in the draft, which was nevertheless tempered by the muslin and silk curtains.

The boudoir was empty, the ball was just beginning, the gaming-tables were open, offering their green cloths and their packs of cards still compressed in the frail case placed upon them by the customs office. The second quadrille was in progress.

All who go to balls will remember that phase of large parties when the guests are not yet all arrived, but when the rooms are already filled —a moment which gives the mistress of the house a transitory pang of terror. This moment is, other points of comparison apart, like that which decides a victory or the loss of a battle.

You will understand, therefore, how what was meant to be a secret now obtains the honors of publicity.

"Well, Caroline?"

"Well, Stephanie?"

"Well?"

"Well?"

A double sigh.

"Have you forgotten our agreement?"

"No."

"Why haven't you been to see me, then?"

"I am never left alone. Even here we shall hardly have time to talk."

"Ah! if Adolphe were to get into such habits as that!" exclaimed Caroline.

"You saw us, Armand and me, when he paid me what is called, I don't know why, his court."

"Yes, I admired him, I thought you very happy, you had found your ideal, a fine, good-sized man, always well dressed, with yellow gloves, his beard well shaven, patent leather boots, a clean shirt, exquisitely neat, and so attentive—"

"Yes, yes, go on."

"In short, quite an elegant man: his voice was femininely sweet, and then such gentleness! And his promises of happiness and liberty! His sentences were veneered with rosewood. He stocked his conversation with shawls and laces. In his smallest expression you heard the rumbling of a coach and four. Your wedding presents were magnificent. Armand seemed to me like a husband of velvet, of a robe of birds' feathers in which you were to be wrapped."

"Caroline, my husband uses tobacco."

"So does mine; that is, he smokes."

"But mine, dear, uses it as they say Napoleon did: in short, he chews, and I hold tobacco in horror. The monster found it out, and went without out it for seven months."

"All men have their habits. They absolutely must use something."

"You have no idea of the tortures I endure. At night I am awakened with a start by one of my own sneezes. As I go to sleep my motions bring the grains of snuff scattered over the pillow under my nose, I inhale, and explode like a mine. It seems that Armand, the wretch, is used to these *surprises*, and doesn't wake up. I find tobacco everywhere, and I certainly didn't marry the customs office."

"But, my dear child, what does this trifling inconvenience amount to, if your husband is kind and possesses a good disposition?"

"He is as cold as marble, as particular as an old bachelor, as communicative as a sentinel; and he's one of those men who say yes to everything, but who never do anything but what they want to."

"Deny him, once."

"I've tried it."

"What came of it?"

"He threatened to reduce my allowance, and to keep back a sum big enough for him to get along without me."

"Poor Stephanie! He's not a man, he's a monster."

"A calm and methodical monster, who wears a scratch, and who, every night—"

"Well, every night—"

"Wait a minute!—who takes a tumbler every night, and puts seven false teeth in it."

"What a trap your marriage was! At any rate, Armand is rich."

"Who knows?"

"Good heavens! Why, you seem to me on the point of becoming very unhappy—or very happy."

"Well, dear, how is it with you?"

"Oh, as for me, I have nothing as yet but a pin that pricks me: but it is intolerable."

"Poor creature! You don't know your own happiness: come, what is it?"

Here the young woman whispered in the other's ear, so that it was impossible to catch a single word. The conversation recommenced, or rather finished by a sort of inference.

"So, your Adolphe is jealous?"

"Jealous of whom? We never leave each other, and that, in itself, is an annoyance. I can't stand it. I don't dare to gape. I am expected to be forever enacting the woman in love. It's fatiguing."

"Caroline?"

"Well?"

"What are you going to do?"

"Resign myself. What are you?

"Fight the customs office."

This little trouble tends to prove that in the matter of personal deception, the two sexes can well cry quits.

DISAPPOINTED AMBITION.

I. CHODOREILLE THE GREAT.

A young man has forsaken his natal city in the depths of one of the departments, rather clearly marked by M. Charles Dupin. He felt that glory of some sort awaited him: suppose that of a painter, a novelist, a journalist, a poet, a great statesman.

Young Adolphe de Chodoreille—that we may be perfectly understood —wished to be talked about, to become celebrated, to be somebody. This, therefore, is addressed to the mass of aspiring individuals brought to Paris by all sorts of vehicles, whether moral or material, and who rush upon the city one fine morning with the hydrophobic purpose of overturning everybody's reputation, and of building themselves a pedestal with the ruins they are to make,— until disenchantment follows. As our intention is to specify this peculiarity so characteristic of our epoch, let us take from among the various personages the one whom the author has elsewhere called *A Distinguished Provencal*.

Adolphe has discovered that the most admirable trade is that which consists in buying a bottle of ink, a bunch of quills, and a ream of paper, at a stationer's for twelve francs and a half, and in selling the two thousand sheets in the ream over again, for something like fifty thousand francs, after having, of course, written upon each leaf fifty lines replete with style and imagination.

This problem,—twelve francs and a half metamorphosed into fifty thousand francs, at the rate of five sous a line—urges numerous families who might advantageously employ their members in the retirement of the provinces, to thrust them into the vortex of Paris.

The young man who is the object of this exportation, invariably passes in his natal town for a man of as much imagination as the most famous author. He has always studied well, he writes very nice poetry, he is considered a fellow of parts: he is besides often guilty of a charming tale published in the local paper, which obtains the admiration of the department.

His poor parents will never know what their son has come to Paris to learn at great cost, namely: That it is difficult to be a writer and to understand the French language short of a dozen years of heculean labor: That a man must have explored every sphere of social life, to become a genuine novelist, inasmuch as the novel is the private history of nations: That the great story-tellers, Aesop, Lucian, Boccaccio, Rabelais, Cervantes, Swift, La Fontaine, Lesage, Sterne, Voltaire, Walter Scott, the unknown Arabians of the *Thousand and One Nights*, were all men of genius as well as giants of erudition.

Their Adolphe serves his literary apprenticeship in two or three coffee-houses, becomes a member of the Society of Men of Letters, attacks, with or without reason, men of talent who don't read his articles, assumes a milder tone on seeing the powerlessness of his criticisms, offers novelettes to the papers which toss them from one to the other as if they were shuttlecocks: and, after five or six years of exercises more or less fatiguing, of dreadful privations which seriously tax his parents, he attains a certain position.

This position may be described as follows: Thanks to a sort of reciprocal support extended to each other, and which an ingenious writer has called "Mutual Admiration," Adolphe often sees his name cited among the names of celebrities, either in the prospectuses of the book-trade, or in the lists of newspapers about to appear. Publishers print the title of one of his works under the deceitful heading "IN PRESS," which might be called the typographical menagerie of bears.* Chodoreille is sometimes mentioned among the promising young men of the literary world.

* A bear (*ours*) is a play which has been refused by a multitude of theatres, but which is finally represented at a time when some manager or other feels the need of one. The word has necessarily passed from the language of the stage into the jargon of journalism, and is applied to novels which wander the streets in search of a publisher.

For eleven years Adolphe Chodoreille remains in the ranks of the promising young men: he finally obtains a free entrance to the theatres, thanks to some dirty work or certain articles of dramatic criticism: he tries to pass for a good fellow; and as he loses his illusions respecting glory and the world of Paris, he gets into debt and his years begin to tell upon him.

A paper which finds itself in a tight place asks him for one of his bears revised by his friends. This has been retouched and revamped every five years, so that it smells of the pomatum of each prevailing and then forgotten fashion. To Adolphe it becomes what the famous cap, which he was constantly staking, was to Corporal Trim, for during five years "Anything for a Woman" (the title decided upon) "will be one of the most entertaining productions of our epoch."

After eleven years, Chodoreille is regarded as having written some respectable things, five or six tales published in the dismal magazines, in ladies' newspapers, or in works intended for children of tender age.

As he is a bachelor, and possesses a coat and a pair of black cassimere trousers, and when he pleases may thus assume the appearance of an elegant diplomat, and as he is not without a certain intelligent air, he is admitted to several more or less literary salons: he bows to the five or six academicians who possess genius, influence or talent, he visits two or three of our great poets, he allows himself, in coffee-rooms, to call the two or three justly celebrated women of our epoch by their Christian names; he is on the best of terms with the blue stockings of the second grade,—who ought to be called *socks*,—and he shakes hands and takes glasses of absinthe with the stars of the smaller newspapers.

Such is the history of every species of ordinary men—men who have been denied what they call good luck. This good luck is nothing less than unyielding will, incessant labor, contempt for an easily won celebrity, immense learning, and that patience which, according to Buffon, is the whole of genius, but which certainly is the half of it.

You do not yet see any indication of a petty trouble for Caroline. You imagine that this history of five hundred young men engaged at this moment in wearing smooth the paving stones of Paris, was written as a sort of warning to the families of the eighty-six departments of France: but read these two letters which lately passed between two girls differently married, and you will see that it was as necessary as the narrative by which every true melodrama was until lately expected to open. You will divine the skillful manoeuvres of the Parisian peacock spreading his tail in the recesses of his native village, and polishing up, for matrimonial purposes, the rays of his glory, which, like those of the sun, are only warm and brilliant at a distance.

From Madame Claire de la Roulandiere, nee Jugault, to Madame Adolphe de Chodoreille, nee Heurtaut.

"VIVIERS.

"You have not yet written to me, and it's real unkind in you. Don't you remember that the happier was to write first and to console her who remained in the country?

"Since your departure for Paris, I have married Monsieur de la Roulandiere, the president of the tribunal. You know him, and you can judge whether I am happy or not, with my heart *saturated*, as it is, with our ideas. I was not ignorant what my lot would be: I live with the ex-president, my husband's uncle, and with my mother-in-law, who has preserved nothing of the ancient parliamentary society of Aix but its pride and its severity of manners. I am seldom alone, I never go out unless accompanied by my mother-in-law or my husband. We receive the heavy people of the city in the evening. They play whist at two sous a point, and I listen to conversations of this nature:

"'Monsieur Vitremont is dead, and leaves two hundred and eighty thousand francs,' says the associate judge, a young man of forty-seven, who is as entertaining as a northwest wind.

"'Are you quite sure of that?'

"The *that* refers to the two hundred and eighty thousand francs. A little judge then holds forth, he runs over the investments, the others discuss their value, and it is definitely settled that if he has not left two hundred and eighty thousand, he left something near it.

"Then comes a universal concert of eulogy heaped upon the dead man's body, for having kept his bread under lock and key, for having shrewdly invested his little savings accumulated sou by sou, in order, probably, that the whole city and those who expect legacies may applaud and exclaim in admiration, 'He leaves two hundred and eighty thousand francs!' Now everybody has rich relations of whom they say 'Will he leave anything like it?' and thus they discuss the quick as they have discussed the dead.

"They talk of nothing but the prospects of fortune, the prospects of a vacancy in office, the prospects of the harvest.

"When we were children, and used to look at those pretty little white mice, in the cobbler's window in the rue St. Maclou, that turned and turned the circular cage in which they were imprisoned, how far I was from thinking that they would one day be a faithful image of my life!

"Think of it, my being in this condition!—I who fluttered my wings so much more than you, I whose imagination was so vagabond! My sins have been greater than yours, and I am the more severely punished. I have bidden farewell to my dreams: I am *Madame la Presidente* in all my glory, and I resign myself to giving my arm for forty years to my big awkward Roulandiere, to living meanly in every way, and to having forever before me two heavy brows and two wall-eyes pierced in a yellow face, which is destined never to know what it is to smile.

"But you, Caroline dear, you who, between ourselves, were admitted among the big girls while I still gamboled among the little ones, you whose only sin was pride, you,—at the age of twenty-seven, and with a dowry of two hundred thousand francs,—capture and captivate a truly great man, one of the wittiest men in Paris, one of the two talented men that our village has produced.—What luck!

"You now circulate in the most brilliant society of Paris. Thanks to the sublime privileges of genius. You may appear in all the salons of the Faubourg St. Germain, and be cordially received. You have the exquisite enjoyment of the company of the two or three celebrated women of our age, where so many good things are said, where the happy speeches which arrive out here like Congreve rockets, are first fired off. You go to the Baron Schinner's of whom Adolphe so often spoke to us, whom all the great artists and foreigners of celebrity visit. In short, before long, you will be one of the queens of Paris, if you wish. You can receive, too, and have at your house the lions of literature, fashion and finance, whether male or female, for Adolphe spoke in such terms about his illustrious friendships and his intimacy with the favorites of the hour, that I imagine you giving and receiving honors.

"With your ten thousand francs a year, and the legacy from your Aunt Carabas, added to the twenty thousand francs that your husband earns, you must keep a carriage; and since you go to all the theatres without paying, since journalists are the heroes of all the inaugurations so ruinous for those who keep up with the movement of Paris, and since they are constantly invited to dinner, you live as if you had an income of sixty thousand francs a year! Happy Caroline! I don't wonder you forget me!

"I can understand how it is that you have not a moment to yourself. Your bliss is the cause of your silence, so I pardon you. Still, if, fatigued with so many pleasures, you one day, upon the summit of your grandeur, think of your poor Claire, write to me, tell me what a marriage with a great man is, describe those great Parisian ladies, especially those who write. Oh! I should *so* much like to know what they are made of! Finally don't forget anything, unless you forget that you are loved, as ever, by your poor

"CLAIRE JUGAULT."

From Madame Adolphe de Chodoreille to Madame la Presidente de la Roulandiere, at Viviers.

"PARIS.

"Ah! my poor Claire, could you have known how many wretched little griefs your innocent letter would awaken, you never would have written it. Certainly no friend, and not even an enemy, on seeing a woman with a thousand mosquito-bites and a plaster over them, would amuse herself by tearing it off and counting the stings.

"I will begin by telling you that for a woman of twenty-seven, with a face still passable, but with a form a little too much like that of the Emperor Nicholas for the humble part I play, I am happy! Let me tell you why: Adolphe, rejoicing in the deceptions which have fallen upon me like a hail-storm, smoothes over the wounds in my self-love by so much affection, so many attentions, and such charming things, that, in good truth, women—so far as they are simply women— would be glad to find in the man they marry defects so advantageous. But all men of letters (Adolphe, alas! is barely a man of letters), who are beings not a bit less irritable, nervous, fickle and eccentric than women, are far from possessing such solid qualities as those of Adolphe, and I hope they have not all been as unfortunate as he.

"Ah! Claire, we love each other well enough for me to tell you the simple truth. I have saved my husband, dear, from profound but skillfully concealed poverty. Far from receiving twenty thousand francs a year, he has not earned that sum in the entire fifteen years that he has been at Paris. We occupy a third story in the rue Joubert, and pay twelve hundred francs for it; we have some eighty-five hundred francs left, with which I endeavor to keep house honorably.

"I have brought Adolphe luck; for since our marriage, he has obtained the control of a feuilleton which is worth four hundred francs a month to him, though it takes but a small portion of his time. He owes this situation to an investment. We employed the seventy thousand francs left me by my Aunt Carabas in giving security for a newspaper; on this we get nine per cent, and we have stock besides. Since this transaction, which was concluded some ten months ago, our income has doubled, and we now possess a competence, I can complain of my marriage in a pecuniary point of view no more than as regards my affections. My vanity alone has suffered, and my ambition has been swamped. You will understand the various petty troubles which have assailed me, by a single specimen.

"Adolphe, you remember, appeared to us on intimate terms with the famous Baroness Schinner, so renowned for her wit, her influence, her wealth and her connection with celebrated men. I supposed that he was welcomed at her house as a friend: my husband presented me, and I was coldly received. I saw that her rooms were furnished with extravagant luxury; and instead of Madame Schinner's returning my call, I received a card, twenty days afterward, and at an insolently improper hour.

"On arriving at Paris, I went to walk upon the boulevard, proud of my anonymous great man. He nudged me with his elbow, and said, pointing out a fat little ill-dressed man, 'There's so and so!' He mentioned one of the seven or eight illustrious men in France. I got ready my look of admiration, and I saw Adolphe rapturously doffing his hat to the truly great man, who replied by the curt little nod that you vouchsafe a person with whom you have doubtless exchanged hardly four words in ten years. Adolphe had begged a look for my sake. 'Doesn't he know you?' I said to my husband. 'Oh, yes, but he probably took me for somebody else,' replied he.

"And so of poets, so of celebrated musicians, so of statesmen. But, as a compensation, we stop and talk for ten minutes in front of some arcade or other, with Messieurs Armand du Cantal, George Beaunoir, Felix Verdoret, of whom you have never heard. Mesdames

Constantine Ramachard, Anais Crottat, and Lucienne Vouillon threaten me with their *blue* friendship. We dine editors totally unknown in our province. Finally I have had the painful happiness of seeing Adolphe decline an invitation to an evening party to which I was not bidden.

"Oh! Claire dear, talent is still the rare flower of spontaneous growth, that no greenhouse culture can produce. I do not deceive myself: Adolphe is an ordinary man, known, estimated as such: he has no other chance, as he himself says, than to take his place among the *utilities* of literature. He was not without wit at Viviers: but to be a man of wit at Paris, you must possess every kind of wit in formidable doses.

"I esteem Adolphe: for, after some few fibs, he frankly confessed his position, and, without humiliating himself too deeply, he promised that I should be happy. He hopes, like numerous other ordinary men, to obtain some place, that of an assistant librarian, for instance, or the pecuniary management of a newspaper. Who knows but we may get him elected deputy for Viviers, in the course of time?

"We live in obscurity; we have five or six friends of either sex whom we like, and such is the brilliant style of life which your letter gilded with all the social splendors.

"From time to time I am caught in a squall, or am the butt of some malicious tongue. Thus, yesterday, at the opera, I heard one of our most ill-natured wits, Leon de Lora, say to one of our most famous critics, 'It takes Chodoreille to discover the Caroline poplar on the banks of the Rhone!' They had heard my husband call me by my Christian name. At Viviers I was considered handsome. I am tall, well made, and fat enough to satisfy Adolphe! In this way I learn that the beauty of women from the country is, at Paris, precisely like the wit of country gentleman.

"In short, I am absolutely nobody, if that is what you wish to know: but if you desire to learn how far my philosophy goes, understand that I am really happy in having found an ordinary man in my pretended great one.

"Farewell, dear Claire! It is still I, you see, who, in spite of my delusions and the petty troubles of my life, am the most favorably situated: for Adolphe is young, and a charming fellow.

"CAROLINE HEURTAUT."

Claire's reply contained, among other passages, the following: "I hope that the indescribable happiness which you enjoy, will continue, thanks to your philosophy." Claire, as any intimate female friend would have done, consoled herself for her president by insinuations respecting Adolphe's prospects and future conduct.

II. ANOTHER GLANCE AT CHODOREILLE.

(Letter discovered one day in a casket, while she was making me wait a long time and trying to get rid of a hanger-on who could not be made to understand hidden meanings. I caught cold—but I got hold of this letter.)

This fatuous note was found on a paper which the notary's clerks had thought of no importance in the inventory of the estate of M. Ferdinand de Bourgarel, who was mourned of late by politics, arts and amours, and in whom is ended the great Provencal house of Borgarelli; for as is generally known the name Bourgarel is a corruption of Borgarelli just as the French Girardin is the Florentine Gherardini.

An intelligent reader will find little difficulty in placing this letter in its proper epoch in the lives of Adolphe and Caroline.

"My dear Friend:

"I thought myself lucky indeed to marry an artist as superior in his talent as in his personal attributes, equally great in soul and mind, worldly-wise, and likely to rise by following the public road without being obliged to wander along crooked, doubtful by-paths. However, you knew Adolphe; you appreciated his worth. I am loved, he is a father, I idolize our children. Adolphe is kindness itself to me; I admire and love him. But, my dear, in this complete happiness lurks a thorn. The roses upon which I recline have more than one fold. In the heart of a woman, folds speedily turn to wounds. These wounds soon bleed, the evil spreads, we suffer, the suffering awakens thoughts, the thoughts swell and change the course of sentiment.

"Ah, my dear, you shall know all about it, though it is a cruel thing to say—but we live as much by vanity as by love. To live by love alone, one must dwell somewhere else than in Paris. What difference would it make to us whether we had only one white percale gown, if the man we love did not see other women dressed differently, more elegantly than we—women who inspire ideas by their ways, by a multitude of little things which really go to make up great passions? Vanity, my dear, is cousin-german to jealousy, to that beautiful and noble jealousy which consists in not allowing one's empire to be invaded, in reigning undisturbed in a soul, and passing one's life happily in a heart.

"Ah, well, my woman's vanity is on the rack. Though some troubles may seem petty indeed, I have learned, unfortunately, that in the home there are no petty troubles. For everything there is magnified by incessant contact with sensations, with desires, with ideas. Such then is the secret of that sadness which you have surprised in me and which I did not care to explain. It is one of those things in which words go too far, and where writing holds at least the thought within bounds by establishing it. The effects of a moral perspective differ so radically between what is said and what is written! All is so solemn, so serious on paper! One cannot commit any more imprudences. Is it not this fact which makes a treasure out of a letter where one gives one's self over to one's thoughts?

"You doubtless thought me wretched, but I am only wounded. You discovered me sitting alone by the fire, and no Adolphe. I had just finished putting the children to bed; they were asleep. Adolphe for the tenth time had been invited out to a house where I do not go, where they want Adolphe without his wife. There are drawing-rooms where he goes without me, just at there are many pleasures in which he alone is the guest. If he were M. de Navarreins and I a d'Espard, society would never think of separating us; it would want us always together. His habits are formed; he does not suspect the humiliation which weighs upon my heart. Indeed, if he had the slightest inkling of this small sorrow which I am ashamed to own, he would drop society, he would become more of a prig than the people who come between us. But he would hamper his progress, he would make enemies, he would raise up obstacles by imposing me upon the salons where I would be subject to a thousand slights. That is why I prefer my sufferings to what would happen were they discovered.

"Adolphe will succeed! He carries my revenge in his beautiful head, does this man of genius. One day the world shall pay for all these slights. But when? Perhaps I shall be forty-five. My beautiful youth will have passed in my chimney-corner, and with this thought: Adolphe smiles, he is enjoying the society of fair women, he is playing the devoted to them, while none of these attentions come my way.

"It may be that these will finally take him from me!

"No one undergoes slight without feeling it, and I feel that I am slighted, though young, beautiful and virtuous. Now, can I keep from thinking this way? Can I control my anger at the thought that Adolphe is dining in the city without me? I take no part in his triumphs; I do not hear the witty or profound remarks made to others! I could no longer be content with bourgeois receptions whence he rescued me, upon finding me *distinguee*, wealthy, young, beautiful and witty. There lies the evil, and it is irremediable.

"In a word, for some cause, it is only since I cannot go to a certain salon that I want to go there. Nothing is more natural of the ways of a human heart. The ancients were wise in having their *gyneceums*. The collisions between the pride of the women, caused by these gatherings, though it dates back only four centuries, has cost our own day much disaffection and numerous bitter debates.

"Be that as it may, my dear, Adolphe is always warmly welcomed when he comes back home. Still, no nature is strong enough to await always with the same ardor. What a morrow that will be, following the evening when his welcome is less warm!

"Now do you see the depth of the fold which I mentioned? A fold in the heart is an abyss, like a crevasse in the Alps—a profundity whose depth and extent we have never been able to calculate. Thus it is between two beings, no matter how near they may be drawn to each other. One never realizes the weight of suffering which oppresses his friend. This seems such a little thing, yet one's life is affected by it in all its length, in all its breadth. I have thus argued with myself; but the more I have argued, the more thoroughly have I realized the extent of this hidden sorrow. And I can only let the current carry me whither it will.

"Two voices struggle for supremacy when—by a rarely fortunate chance —I am alone in my armchair waiting for Adolphe. One, I would wager, comes from Eugene Delacroix's *Faust* which I have on my table. Mephistopheles speaks, that terrible aide who guides the swords so dexterously. He leaves the engraving, and places himself diabolically before me, grinning through the hole which the great artist has placed under his nose, and gazing at me with that eye whence fall rubies, diamonds, carriages, jewels, laces, silks, and a thousand luxuries to feed the burning desire within me.

"'Are you not fit for society?' he asks. 'You are the equal of the fairest duchesses. Your voice is like a siren's, your hands command respect and love. Ah! that arm!—place bracelets upon it, and how pleasingly it would rest upon the velvet of a robe! Your locks are chains which would fetter all men. And you could lay all your triumphs at Adolphe's feet, show him your power and never use it. Then he would fear, where now he lives in insolent certainty. Come! To action! Inhale a few mouthfuls of disdain and you will exhale clouds of incense. Dare to reign! Are you not next to nothing here in your chimney-corner? Sooner or later the pretty spouse, the beloved wife will die, if you continue like this, in a dressing-gown. Come, and you shall perpetuate your sway through the arts of coquetry! Show yourself in salons, and your pretty foot shall trample down the love of your rivals.'

"The other voice comes from my white marble mantel, which rustles like a garment. I think I see a veritable goddess crowned with white roses, and bearing a palm-branch in her hand. Two blue eyes smile down on me. This simple image of virtue says to me:

"'Be content! Remain good always, and make this man happy. That is the whole of your mission. The sweetness of angels triumphs over all pain. Faith in themselves has enabled the martyrs to obtain solace even on the brasiers of their tormentors. Suffer a moment; you shall be happy in the end.'

"Sometimes Adolphe enters at that moment and I am content. But, my dear, I have less patience than love. I almost wish to tear in pieces the woman who can go everywhere, and whose society is sought out by men and women alike. What profound thought lies in the line of Moliere:

"'The world, dear Agnes, is a curious thing!'

"You know nothing of this petty trouble, you fortunate Mathilde! You are well born. You can do a great deal for me. Just think! I can write you things that I dared not speak about. Your visits mean so much; come often to see your poor

"Caroline."

"Well," said I to the notary's clerk, "do you know what was the nature of this letter to the late Bourgarel?"

"No."

"A note of exchange."

Neither clerk nor notary understood my meaning. Do you?

THE PANGS OF INNOCENCE.

"Yes, dear, in the married state, many things will happen to you which you are far from expecting: but then others will happen which you expect still less. For instance—"

The author (may we say the ingenious author?) *qui castigat ridendo mores*, and who has undertaken the *Petty Troubles of Married Life*, hardly needs to remark, that, for prudence' sake, he here allows a lady of high distinction to speak, and that he does not assume the responsibility of her language, though he professes the most sincere admiration for the charming person to whom he owes his acquaintance with this petty trouble.

"For instance—" she says.

He nevertheless thinks proper to avow that this person is neither Madame Foullepointe, nor Madame de Fischtaminel, nor Madame Deschars.

Madame Deschars is too prudish, Madame Foullepointe too absolute in her household, and she knows it; indeed, what doesn't she know? She is good-natured, she sees good society, she wishes to have the best: people overlook the vivacity of her witticisms, as, under louis XIV, they overlooked the remarks of Madame Cornuel. They overlook a good many things in her; there are some women who are the spoiled children of public opinion.

As to Madame de Fischtaminel, who is, in fact, connected with the affair, as you shall see, she, being unable to recriminate, abstains from words and recriminates in acts.

We give permission to all to think that the speaker is Caroline herself, not the silly little Caroline of tender years. But Caroline when she has become a woman of thirty.

"For instance," she remarks to a young woman whom she is edifying, "you will have children, God willing."

"Madame," I say, "don't let us mix the deity up in this, unless it is an allusion—"

111

"You are impertinent," she replies, "you shouldn't interrupt a woman—"

"When she is busy with children, I know: but, madame, you ought not to trifle with the innocence of young ladies. Mademoiselle is going to be married, and if she were led to count upon the intervention of the Supreme Being in this affair, she would fall into serious errors. We should not deceive the young. Mademoiselle is beyond the age when girls are informed that their little brother was found under a cabbage."

"You evidently want to get me confused," she replies, smiling and showing the loveliest teeth in the world. "I am not strong enough to argue with you, so I beg you to let me go on with Josephine. What was I saying?"

"That if I get married, I shall have children," returns the young lady.

"Very well. I will not represent things to you worse than they are, but it is extremely probable that each child will cost you a tooth. With every baby I have lost a tooth."

"Happily," I remark at this, "this trouble was with you less than petty, it was positively nothing."—They were side teeth.—"But take notice, miss, that this vexation has no absolute, unvarying character as such. The annoyance depends upon the condition of the tooth. If the baby causes the loss of a decayed tooth, you are fortunate to have a baby the more and a bad tooth the less. Don't let us confound blessings with bothers. Ah! if you were to lose one of your magnificent front teeth, that would be another thing! And yet there is many a woman that would give the best tooth in her head for a fine, healthy boy!"

"Well," resumes Caroline, with animation, "at the risk of destroying your illusions, poor child, I'll just show you a petty trouble that counts! Ah, it's atrocious! And I won't leave the subject of dress which this gentleman considers the only subject we women are equal to."

I protest by a gesture.

"I had been married about two years," continues Caroline, "and I loved my husband. I have got over it since and acted differently for

112

his happiness and mine. I can boast of having one of the happiest homes in Paris. In short, my dear, I loved the monster, and, even when out in society, saw no one but him. My husband had already said to me several times, 'My dear, young women never dress well; your mother liked to have you look like a stick, —she had her reasons for it. If you care for my advice, take Madame de Fischtaminel for a model: she is a lady of taste.' I, unsuspecting creature that I was, saw no perfidy in the recommendation.

"One evening as we returned from a party, he said, 'Did you notice how Madame de Fischtaminel was dressed!' 'Yes, very neatly.' And I said to myself, 'He's always talking about Madame de Fischtaminel; I must really dress just like her.' I had noticed the stuff and the make of the dress, and the style of the trimmings. I was as happy as could be, as I went trotting about town, doing everything I could to obtain the same articles. I sent for the very same dressmaker.

"'You work for Madame de Fischtaminel,' I said.

"'Yes, madame.'

"'Well, I will employ you as my dressmaker, but on one condition: you see I have procured the stuff of which her gown is made, and I want you to make me one exactly like it.'

"I confess that I did not at first pay any attention to a rather shrewd smile of the dressmaker, though I saw it and afterwards accounted for it. 'So like it,' I added, 'that you can't tell them apart.'

"Oh," says Caroline, interrupting herself and looking at me, "you men teach us to live like spiders in the depths of their webs, to see everything without seeming to look at it, to investigate the meaning and spirit of words, movements, looks. You say, 'How cunning women are!' But you should say, 'How deceitful men are!'

"I can't tell you how much care, how many days, how many manoeuvres, it cost me to become Madame de Fischtaminel's duplicate! But these are our battles, child," she adds, returning to Josephine. "I could not find a certain little embroidered neckerchief, a very marvel! I finally learned that it was made to order. I unearthed the embroideress, and ordered a kerchief like Madame de Fischtaminel's. The price was a mere trifle, one hundred and fifty francs! It had been ordered by a gentleman who had made a present of it to Madame de Fischtaminel. All my savings were absorbed by it. Now we women of Paris are all of us very much restricted in the article of dress. There is not a man worth a hundred thousand francs a year, that loses ten thousand a winter at whist, who does not consider his wife extravagant, and is not alarmed at her bills for what he calls 'rags'! 'Let my savings go,' I said. And they went. I had the modest pride of a woman in love: I would not speak a word to Adolphe of my dress; I wanted it to be a surprise, goose that I was! Oh, how brutally you men take away our blessed ignorance!"

This remark is meant for me, for me who had taken nothing from the lady, neither tooth, nor anything whatever of the things with a name and without a name that may be taken from a woman.

"I must tell you that my husband took me to Madame de Fischtaminel's, where I dined quite often. I heard her say to him, 'Why, your wife looks very well!' She had a patronizing way with me that I put up with: Adolphe wished that I could have her wit and preponderance in society. In short, this phoenix of women was my model. I studied and copied her, I took immense pains not to be myself—oh!—it was a poem that no one but us women can understand! Finally, the day of my triumph dawned. My heart beat for joy, as if I were a child, as if I were what we all are at twenty-two. My husband was going to call for me for a walk in the Tuileries: he came in, I looked at him radiant with joy, but he took no notice. Well, I can confess it now, it was one of those frightful disasters—but I will say nothing about it —this gentleman here would make fun of me."

I protest by another movement.

"It was," she goes on, for a woman never stops till she has told the whole of a thing, "as if I had seen an edifice built by a fairy crumble into ruins. Adolphe manifested not the slightest surprise. We got into the carriage. Adolphe noticed my sadness, and asked me what the matter was: I replied as we always do when our hearts are wrung by these petty vexations, 'Oh, nothing!' Then he took his eye-glass, and stared at the promenaders on the Champs Elysees, for we were to go the rounds of the Champs Elysees, before taking our walk at the Tuileries. Finally, a fit of impatience seized me. I felt a slight attack of fever, and when I got home, I composed myself to smile. 'You haven't said a word about my dress!' I muttered. 'Ah, yes, your gown is somewhat like Madame de Fischtaminel's.' He turned on his heel and went away.

"The next day I pouted a little, as you may readily imagine. Just as we were finishing breakfast by the fire in my room—I shall never forget it—the embroideress called to get her money for the neckerchief. I paid her. She bowed to my husband as if she knew him. I ran after her on pretext of getting her to receipt the bill, and said: 'You didn't ask *him* so much for Madame de Fischtaminel's kerchief!' 'I assure you, madame, it's the same price, the gentleman did not beat me down a mite.' I returned to my room where I found my husband looking as foolish as—"

She hesitates and then resumes: "As a miller just made a bishop. 'I understand, love, now, that I shall never be anything more than *somewhat like* Madame de Fischtaminel.' 'You refer to her neckerchief, I suppose: well, I *did* give it to her,—it was for her birthday. You see, we were formerly—' 'Ah, you were formerly more intimate than you are now!' Without replying to this, he added, '*But it's altogether moral.*'

"He took his hat and went out, leaving me with this fine declaration of the Rights of Man. He did not return and came home late at night. I remained in my chamber and wept like a Magdalen, in the chimney-corner. You may laugh at me, if you will," she adds, looking at me, "but I shed tears over my youthful illusions, and I wept, too, for spite, at having been taken for a dupe. I remembered the dressmaker's smile! Ah, that smile reminded me of the smiles of a number of women, who laughed at seeing me so innocent and unsuspecting at Madame de Fischtaminel's! I wept sincerely. Until now I had a right to give my husband credit for many things which he did not possess, but in the existence of which young married women pertinaciously believe.

"How many great troubles are included in this petty one! You men are a vulgar set. There is not a woman who does not carry her delicacy so far as to embroider her past life with the most delightful fibs, while you—but I have had my revenge."

"Madame," I say, "you are giving this young lady too much information."

"True," she returns, "I will tell you the sequel some other time."

"Thus, you see, mademoiselle," I say, "you imagine you are buying a neckerchief and you find a *petty trouble* round your neck: if you get it given to you—"

"It's a *great* trouble," retorts the woman of distinction. "Let us stop here."

The moral of this fable is that you must wear your neckerchief without thinking too much about it. The ancient prophets called this world, even in their time, a valley of woe. Now, at that period, the Orientals had, with the permission of the constituted authorities, a swarm of comely slaves, besides their wives! What shall we call the valley of the Seine between Calvary and Charenton, where the law allows but one lawful wife.

THE UNIVERSAL AMADIS.

You will understand at once that I began to gnaw the head of my cane, to consult the ceiling, to gaze at the fire, to examine Caroline's foot, and I thus held out till the marriageable young lady was gone.

"You must excuse me," I said, "if I have remained behind, perhaps in spite of you: but your vengeance would lose by being recounted by and by, and if it constituted a petty trouble for your husband, I have the greatest interest in hearing it, and you shall know why."

"Ah," she returned, "that expression, '*it's altogether moral,*' which he gave as an excuse, shocked me to the last degree. It was a great consolation, truly, to me, to know that I held the place, in his household, of a piece of furniture, a block; that my kingdom lay among the kitchen utensils, the accessories of my toilet, and the physicians' prescriptions; that our conjugal love had been assimilated to dinner pills, to veal soup and white mustard; that Madame de Fischtaminel possessed my husband's soul, his admiration, and that she charmed and satisfied his intellect, while I was a kind of purely physical necessity! What do you think of a woman's being degraded to the situation of a soup or a plate of boiled beef, and without parsley, at that! Oh, I composed a catilinic, that evening—"

"Philippic is better."

"Well, either. I'll say anything you like, for I was perfectly furious, and I don't remember what I screamed in the desert of my bedroom. Do you suppose that this opinion that husbands have of their wives, the parts they give them, is not a singular vexation for us? Our petty troubles are always pregnant with greater ones. My Adolphe needed a lesson. You know the Vicomte de Lustrac, a desperate amateur of women and music, an epicure, one of those ex-beaux of the Empire, who live upon their earlier successes, and who cultivate themselves with excessive care, in order to secure a second crop?"

"Yes," I said, "one of those laced, braced, corseted old fellows of sixty, who work such wonders by the grace of their forms, and who might give a lesson to the youngest dandies among us."

"Monsieur de Lustrac is as selfish as a king, but gallant and pretentious, spite of his jet black wig."

"As to his whiskers, he dyes them."

"He goes to ten parties in an evening: he's a butterfly."

"He gives capital dinners and concerts, and patronizes inexperienced songstresses."

"He takes bustle for pleasure."

"Yes, but he makes off with incredible celerity whenever a misfortune occurs. Are you in mourning, he avoids you. Are you confined, he awaits your churching before he visits you. He possesses a mundane frankness and a social intrepidity which challenge admiration."

"But does it not require courage to appear to be what one really is?" I asked.

"Well," she resumed, after we had exchanged our observations on this point, "this young old man, this universal Amadis, whom we call among ourselves Chevalier *Petit-Bon-Homme-vil-encore*, became the object of my admiration. I made him a few of those advances which never compromise a woman; I spoke of the good taste exhibited in his latest waistcoats and in his canes, and he thought me a lady of extreme amiability. I thought him a chevalier of extreme youth; he called upon me; I put on a number of little airs, and pretended to be unhappy at home, and to have deep sorrows. You know what a woman means when she talks of her sorrows, and complains that she is not understood. The old ape replied much better than a young man would, and I had the greatest difficulty in keeping a straight face while I listened to him.

"'Ah, that's the way with husbands, they pursue the very worst polity, they respect their wives, and, sooner or later, every woman is enraged at finding herself respected, and divines the secret education to which she is entitled. Once married, you ought not to live like a little school-girl, etc.'

"As he spoke, he leaned over me, he squirmed, he was horrible to see. He looked like a wooden Nuremberg doll, he stuck out his chin, he stuck out his chair, he stuck out his hand—in short, after a variety of marches and countermarches, of declarations that were perfectly angelic—"

"No!"

"Yes. *Petit-Bon-Homme-vil-encore* had abandoned the classicism of his youth for the romanticism now in fashion: he spoke of the soul, of angels, of adoration, of submission, he became ethereal, and of the darkest blue. He took me to the opera, and handed me to my carriage. This old young man went when I went, his waistcoats multiplied, he compressed his waist, he excited his horse to a gallop in order to catch and accompany my carriage to the promenade: he compromised me with the grace of a young collegian, and was considered madly in love with me. I was steadfastly cruel, but accepted his arm and his bouquets. We were talked about. I was delighted, and managed before long to be surprised by my husband, with the viscount on the sofa in my boudoir, holding my hands in his, while I listened in a sort of external ecstasy. It is incredible how much a desire for vengeance will induce us to put up with! I appeared vexed at the entrance of my husband, who made a scene on the viscount's departure: 'I assure you, sir,' said I, after having listened to his reproaches, 'that *it's altogether moral.*' My husband saw the point and went no more to Madame de Fischtaminel's. I received Monsieur de Lustrac no more, either."

"But," I interrupted, "this Lustrac that you, like many others, take for a bachelor, is a widower, and childless."

"Really!"

"No man ever buried his wife deeper than he buried his: she will hardly be found at the day of judgment. He married before the Revolution, and your *altogether moral* reminds me of a speech of his that I shall have to repeat for your benefit. Napoleon appointed Lustrac to an important office, in a conquered province. Madame de Lustrac, abandoned for governmental duties, took a private secretary for her private affairs, though it was altogether moral: but she was wrong in selecting him without informing her husband. Lustrac met this secretary in a state of some excitement, in consequence of a lively discussion in his wife's chamber, and at an exceedingly early hour in the morning. The city desired nothing better than to laugh at its governor, and this adventure made such a sensation that Lustrac himself begged the Emperor to recall him. Napoleon desired his representatives to be men of morality, and he held that such disasters as this must inevitably take from a man's consideration. You know that among the Emperor's unhappy passions, was that of reforming his court and his government. Lustrac's request was granted, therefore, but without compensation. When he returned to Paris, he reappeared at his mansion, with his wife; he took her into society—a step which is certainly conformable to the most refined habits of the aristocracy —but then there are always people who want to find out about it. They inquired the reason of this chivalrous championship. 'So you are reconciled, you and Madame de Lustrac,' some one said to him in the lobby of the Emperor's theatre, 'you have pardoned her, have you? So much the better.' 'Oh,' replied he, with a satisfied air, 'I became convinced—' 'Ah, that she was innocent, very good.' 'No, I became convinced that it was altogether physical.'"

Caroline smiled.

"The opinion of your admirer reduced this weighty trouble to what is, in this case as in yours, a very petty one."

"A petty trouble!" she exclaimed, "and pray for what do you take the fatigue of coquetting with a de Lustrac, of whom I have made an enemy! Ah, women often pay dearly enough for the bouquets they receive and the attentions they accept. Monsieur de Lustrac said of me to Monsieur de Bourgarel, 'I would not advise you to pay court to that woman; she is too dear.'"

WITHOUT AN OCCUPATION.

"PARIS, 183-

"You ask me, dear mother, whether I am happy with my husband. Certainly Monsieur de Fischtaminel was not the ideal of my dreams. I submitted to your will, as you know. His fortune, that supreme consideration, spoke, indeed, sufficiently loud. With these arguments, —a marriage, without stooping, with the Count de Fischtaminel, his having thirty thousand a year, and a home at Paris—you were strongly armed against your poor daughter. Besides, Monsieur de Fischtaminel is good looking for a man of thirty-six years; he received the cross of the Legion of Honor from Napoleon upon the field of battle, he is an ex-colonel, and had it not been for the Restoration, which put him upon half-pay, he would be a general. These are certainly extenuating circumstances.

"Many women consider that I have made a good match, and I am bound to confess that there is every appearance of happiness,—for the public, that is. But you will acknowledge that if you had known of the return of my Uncle Cyrus and of his intention to leave me his money, you would have given me the privilege of choosing for myself.

"I have nothing to say against Monsieur de Fischtaminel: he does not gamble, he is indifferent to women, he doesn't like wine, and he has no expensive fancies: he possesses, as you said, all the negative qualities which make husbands passable. Then, what is the matter with him? Well, mother, he has nothing to do. We are together the whole blessed day! Would you believe that it is during the night, when we are the most closely united, that I am the most alone? His sleep is my asylum, my liberty begins when he slumbers. This state of siege will yet make me sick: I am never alone. If Monsieur de Fischtaminel were jealous, I should have a resource. There would then be a struggle, a comedy: but how could the aconite of jealousy have taken root in his soul? He has never left me since our marriage. He feels no shame in stretching himself out upon a sofa and remaining there for hours together.

"Two felons pinioned to the same chain do not find time hang heavy: for they have their escape to think of. But we have no subject of conversation; we have long since talked ourselves out. A little while ago he was so far reduced as to talk politics. But even politics are exhausted, Napoleon, unfortunately for me, having died at St. Helena, as is well known.

"Monsieur de Fischtaminel abhors reading. If he sees me with a book, he comes and says a dozen times an hour—'Nina, dear, haven't you finished yet?'

"I endeavored to persuade this innocent persecutor to ride out every day on horseback, and I alleged a consideration usually conclusive with men of forty years,—his health! But he said that after having been twelve years on horseback, he felt the need of repose.

"My husband, dear mother, is a man who absorbs you, he uses up the vital fluid of his neighbor, his ennui is gluttonous: he likes to be amused by those who call upon us, and, after five years of wedlock, no one ever comes: none visit us but those whose intentions are evidently dishonorable for him, and who endeavor, unsuccessfully, to amuse him, in order to earn the right to weary his wife.

"Monsieur de Fischtaminel, mother, opens the door of my chamber, or of the room to which I have flown for refuge, five or six times an hour, and comes up to me in an excited way, and says, 'Well, what are you doing, my belle?' (the expression in fashion during the Empire) without perceiving that he is constantly repeating the same phrase, which is to me like the one pint too much that the executioner formerly poured into the torture by water.

"Then there's another bore! We can't go to walk any more. A promenade without conversation, without interest, is impossible. My husband walks with me for the walk, as if he were alone. I have the fatigue without the pleasure.

"The interval between getting up and breakfast is employed in my toilet, in my household duties; and I manage to get through with this part of the day. But between breakfast and dinner, there is a whole desert to plough, a waste to traverse. My husband's want of occupation does not leave me a moment of repose, he overpowers me by his uselessness; his idle life positively wears me out. His two eyes always open and gazing at mine compel me to keep them lowered. Then his monotonous remarks:

"'What o'clock is it, love? What are you doing now? What are you thinking of? What do you mean to do? Where shall we go this evening? Anything new? What weather! I don't feel well, etc., etc.'

"All these variations upon the same theme—the interrogation point —which compose Fischtaminel's repertory, will drive me mad. Add to these leaden arrows everlastingly shot off at me, one last trait which will complete the description of my happiness, and you will understand my life.

"Monsieur de Fischtaminel, who went away in 1809, with the rank of sub-lieutenant, at the age of eighteen, has had no other education than that due to discipline, to the natural sense of honor of a noble and a soldier: but though he possesses tact, the sentiment of probity, and a proper subordination, his ignorance is gross, he knows absolutely nothing, and he has a horror of learning anything. Oh, dear mother, what an accomplished door-keeper this colonel would have made, had he been born in indigence! I don't think a bit the better of him for his bravery, for he did not fight against the Russians, the Austrians, or the Prussians: he fought against ennui. When he rushed upon the enemy, Captain Fischtaminel's purpose was to get away from himself. He married because he had nothing else to do.

"We have another slight difficulty to content with: my husband harasses the servants to such a degree that we change them every six months.

"I so ardently desire, dear mother, to remain a virtuous woman, that I am going to try the effect of traveling for half the year. During the winter, I shall go every evening to the Italian or the French opera, or to parties: but I don't know whether our fortune will permit such an expenditure. Uncle Cyrus ought to come to Paris—I would take care of him as I would of an inheritance.

"If you discover a cure for my woes, let your daughter know of it — your daughter who loves you as much as she deplores her misfortunes, and who would have been glad to call herself by some other name than that of

"NINA FISCHTAMINEL."

Besides the necessity of describing this petty trouble, which could only be described by the pen of a woman,—and what a woman she was! —it was necessary to make you acquainted with a character whom you saw only in profile in the first half of this book, the queen of the particular set in which Caroline lived,—a woman both envied and adroit, who succeeded in conciliating, at an early date, what she owed to the world with the requirements of the heart. This letter is her absolution.

INDISCRETIONS.

Women are either chaste—or vain—or simply proud. They are therefore all subject to the following petty trouble:

Certain husbands are so delighted to have, in the form of a wife, a woman to themselves,—a possession exclusively due to the legal ceremony,—that they dread the public's making a mistake, and they hasten to brand their consort, as lumber-dealers brand their logs while floating down stream, or as the Berry stock-raisers brand their sheep. They bestow names of endearment, right before people, upon their wives: names taken, after the Roman fashion (columbella), from the animal kingdom, as: my chick, my duck, my dove, my lamb; or, choosing from the vegetable kingdom, they call them: my cabbage, my fig (this only in Provence), my plum (this only in Alsatia). Never: —My flower! Pray note this discretion.

Or else, which is more serious, they call their wives:—Bobonne, — mother,—daughter,—good woman,—old lady: this last when she is very young.

Some venture upon names of doubtful propriety, such as: Mon bichon, ma niniche, Tronquette!

We once heard one of our politicians, a man extremely remarkable for his ugliness, call his wife, *Moumoutte!*

"I would rather he would strike me," said this unfortunate to her neighbor.

"Poor little woman, she is really unhappy," resumed the neighbor, looking at me when Moumoutte had gone: "when she is in company with her husband she is upon pins and needles, and keeps out of his way. One evening, he actually seized her by the neck and said: 'Come fatty, let's go home!'"

It has been alleged that the cause of a very famous husband-poisoning with arsenic, was nothing less than a series of constant indiscretions like these that the wife had to bear in society. This husband used to give the woman he had won at the point of the Code, public little taps on her shoulder, he would startle her by a resounding kiss, he dishonored her by a conspicuous tenderness, seasoned by those impertinent attentions the secret of which belongs to the French savages who dwell in the depths of the provinces, and whose manners are very little known, despite the efforts of the realists in fiction. It was, it is said, this shocking situation,—one perfectly appreciated by a discerning jury,—which won the prisoner a verdict softened by the extenuating circumstances.

The jurymen said to themselves:

"For a wife to murder her husband for these conjugal offences, is certainly going rather far; but then a woman is very excusable, when she is so harassed!"

We deeply regret, in the interest of elegant manners, that these arguments are not more generally known. Heaven grant, therefore, that our book may have an immense success, as women will obtain this advantage from it, that they will be treated as they deserve, that is, as queens.

In this respect, love is much superior to marriage, it is proud of indiscreet sayings and doings. There are some women that seek them, fish for them, and woe to the man who does not now and then commit one!

What passion lies in an accidental *thou*!

Out in the country I heard a husband call his wife: "Ma berline!" She was delighted with it, and saw nothing ridiculous in it: she called her husband, "Mon fiston!" This delicious couple were ignorant of the existence of such things as petty troubles.

It was in observing this happy pair that the author discovered this axiom:

Axiom:—In order to be happy in wedlock, you must either be a man of genius married to an affectionate and intellectual woman, or, by a chance which is not as common as might be supposed, you must both of you be exceedingly stupid.

The too celebrated history of the cure of a wounded self-love by arsenic, proves that, properly speaking, there are no petty troubles for women in married life.

126

Axiom.—Woman exists by sentiment where man exists by action.

Now, sentiment can at any moment render a petty trouble either a great misfortune, or a wasted life, or an eternal misery. Should Caroline begin, in her ignorance of life and the world, by inflicting upon her husband the vexations of her stupidity (re-read REVELATIONS), Adolphe, like any other man, may find a compensation in social excitement: he goes out, comes back, goes here and there, has business. But for Caroline, the question everywhere is, To love or not to love, to be or not to be loved.

Indiscretions are in harmony with the character of the individuals, with times and places. Two examples will suffice.

Here is the first. A man is by nature dirty and ugly: he is ill-made and repulsive. There are men, and often rich ones, too, who, by a sort of unobserved constitution, soil a new suit of clothes in twenty-four hours. They were born disgusting. It is so disgraceful for a women to be anything more than just simply a wife to this sort of Adolphe, that a certain Caroline had long ago insisted upon the suppression of the modern *thee* and *thou* and all other insignia of the wifely dignity. Society had been for five or six years accustomed to this sort of thing, and supposed Madame and Monsieur completely separated, and all the more so as it had noticed the accession of a Ferdinand II.

One evening, in the presence of a dozen persons, this man said to his wife: "Caroline, hand me the tongs, there's a love." It is nothing, and yet everything. It was a domestic revelation.

Monsieur de Lustrac, the Universal Amadis, hurried to Madame de Fischtaminel's, narrated this little scene with all the spirit at his command, and Madame de Fischtaminel put on an air something like Celimene's and said: "Poor creature, what an extremity she must be in!"

I say nothing of Caroline's confusion,—you have already divined it.

Here is the second. Think of the frightful situation in which a lady of great refinement was lately placed: she was conversing agreeably at her country seat near Paris, when her husband's servant came and whispered in her ear, "Monsieur has come, madame."

"Very well, Benoit."

Everybody had heard the rumblings of the vehicle. It was known that the husband had been at Paris since Monday, and this took place on Saturday, at four in the afternoon.

"He's got something important to say to you, madame."

Though this dialogue was held in a whisper, it was perfectly understood, and all the more so from the fact that the lady of the house turned from the pale hue of the Bengal rose to the brilliant crimson of the wheatfield poppy. She nodded and went on with the conversation, and managed to leave her company on the pretext of learning whether her husband had succeeded in an important undertaking or not: but she seemed plainly vexed at Adolphe's want of consideration for the company who were visiting her.

During their youth, women want to be treated as divinities, they love the ideal; they cannot bear the idea of being what nature intended them to be.

Some husbands, on retiring to the country, after a week in town, are worse than this: they bow to the company, put their arm round their wife's waist, take a little walk with her, appear to be talking confidentially, disappear in a clump of trees, get lost, and reappear half an hour afterward.

This, ladies, is a genuine petty trouble for a young woman, but for a woman beyond forty, this sort of indiscretion is so delightful, that the greatest prudes are flattered by it, for, be it known:

That women of a certain age, women on the shady side, want to be treated as mortals, they love the actual; they cannot bear the idea of no longer being what nature intended them to be.

Axiom.—Modesty is a relative virtue; there is the modesty of the woman of twenty, the woman of thirty, the woman of forty-five.

Thus the author said to a lady who told him to guess at her age: "Madame, yours is the age of indiscretion."

This charming woman of thirty-nine was making a Ferdinand much too conspicuous, while her daughter was trying to conceal her Ferdinand I.

BRUTAL DISCLOSURES.

FIRST STYLE. Caroline adores Adolphe, she thinks him handsome, she thinks him superb, especially in his National Guard uniform. She starts when a sentinel presents arms to him, she considers him moulded like a model, she regards him as a man of wit, everything he does is right, nobody has better taste than he, in short, she is crazy about Adolphe.

It's the old story of Cupid's bandage. This is washed every ten years, and newly embroidered by the altered manners of the period, but it has been the same old bandage since the days of Greece.

Caroline is at a ball with one of her young friends. A man well known for his bluntness, whose acquaintance she is to make later in life, but whom she now sees for the first time, Monsieur Foullepointe, has commenced a conversation with Caroline's friend. According to the custom of society, Caroline listens to this conversation without mingling in it.

"Pray tell me, madame," says Monsieur Foullepointe, "who is that queer man who has been talking about the Court of Assizes before a gentleman whose acquittal lately created such a sensation: he is all the while blundering, like an ox in a bog, against everybody's sore spot. A lady burst into tears at hearing him tell of the death of a child, as she lost her own two months ago."

"Who do you mean?"

"Why, that fat man, dressed like a waiter in a cafe, frizzled like a barber's apprentice, there, he's trying now to make himself agreeable to Madame de Fischtaminel."

"Hush," whispers the lady quite alarmed, "it's the husband of the little woman next to me!"

"Ah, it's your husband?" says Monsieur Foullepointe. "I am delighted, madame, he's a charming man, so vivacious, gay and witty. I am going to make his acquaintance immediately."

And Foullepointe executes his retreat, leaving a bitter suspicion in Caroline's soul, as to the question whether her husband is really as handsome as she thinks him.

SECOND STYLE. Caroline, annoyed by the reputation of Madame Schinner, who is credited with the possession of epistolary talents, and styled the "Sevigne of the note", tired of hearing about Madame de Fischtaminel, who has ventured to write a little 32mo book on the education of the young, in which she has boldly reprinted Fenelon, without the style:—Caroline has been working for six months upon a tale tenfold poorer than those of Berquin, nauseatingly moral, and flamboyant in style.

After numerous intrigues such as women are skillful in managing in the interest of their vanity, and the tenacity and perfection of which would lead you to believe that they have a third sex in their head, this tale, entitled "The Lotus," appears in three installments in a leading daily paper. It is signed Samuel Crux.

When Adolphe takes up the paper at breakfast, Caroline's heart beats up in her very throat: she blushes, turns pale, looks away and stares at the ceiling. When Adolphe's eyes settle upon the feuilleton, she can bear it no longer: she gets up, goes out, comes back, having replenished her stock of audacity, no one knows where.

"Is there a feuilleton this morning?" she asks with an air that she thinks indifferent, but which would disturb a husband still jealous of his wife.

"Yes, one by a beginner, Samuel Crux. The name is a disguise, clearly: the tale is insignificant enough to drive an insect to despair, if he could read: and vulgar, too: the style is muddy, but then it's—"

Caroline breathes again. "It's—" she suggests.

"It's incomprehensible," resumes Adolphe. "Somebody must have paid Chodoreille five or six hundred francs to insert it; or else it's the production of a blue-stocking in high society who has promised to invite Madame Chodoreille to her house; or perhaps it's the work of a woman in whom the editor is personally interested. Such a piece of stupidity cannot be explained any other way. Imagine, Caroline, that it's all about a little flower picked on the edge of a wood in a sentimental walk, which a gentleman of the Werther school has sworn to keep, which he has had framed, and which the lady claims again eleven years after (the poor man has had time to change his lodgings three times). It's quite new, about as old as Sterne or Gessner. What makes me think it's a woman, is that the first literary idea of the whole sex is to take vengeance on some one."

Adolphe might go on pulling "The Lotus" to pieces; Caroline's ears are full of the tinkling of bells. She is like the woman who threw herself over the Pont des Arts, and tried to find her way ten feet below the level of the Seine.

ANOTHER STYLE. Caroline, in her paroxysms of jealousy, has discovered a hiding place used by Adolphe, who, as he can't trust his wife, and as he knows she opens his letters and rummages in his drawers, has endeavored to save his correspondence with Hector from the hooked fingers of the conjugal police.

Hector is an old schoolmate, who has married in the Loire Inferieure.

Adolphe lifts up the cloth of his writing desk, a cloth the border of which has been embroidered by Caroline, the ground being blue, black or red velvet,—the color, as you see, is perfectly immaterial,— and he slips his unfinished letters to Madame de Fischtaminel, to his friend Hector, between the table and the cloth.

The thickness of a sheet of paper is almost nothing, velvet is a downy, discreet material, but, no matter, these precautions are in vain. The male devil is fairly matched by the female devil: Tophet will furnish them of all genders. Caroline has Mephistopheles on her side, the demon who causes tables to spurt forth fire, and who, with his ironic finger points out the hiding place of keys—the secret of secrets.

Caroline has noticed the thickness of a letter sheet between this velvet and this table: she hits upon a letter to Hector instead of hitting upon one to Madame de Fischtaminel, who has gone to Plombieres Springs, and reads the following:

"My dear Hector:

"I pity you, but you have acted wisely in entrusting me with a knowledge of the difficulties in which you have voluntarily involved yourself. You never would see the difference between the country woman and the woman of Paris. In the country, my dear boy, you are always face to face with your wife, and, owing to the ennui which impels you, you rush headforemost into the enjoyment of your bliss. This is a great error: happiness is an abyss, and when you have once reached the bottom, you never get back again, in wedlock.

"I will show you why. Let me take, for your wife's sake, the shortest path—the parable.

"I remember having made a journey from Paris to Ville-Parisis, in that vehicle called a 'bus: distance, twenty miles: 'bus, lumbering: horse, lame. Nothing amuses me more than to draw from people, by the aid of that gimlet called the interrogation, and to obtain, by means of an attentive air, the sum of information, anecdotes and learning that everybody is anxious to part with: and all men have such a sum, the peasant as well as the banker, the corporal as well as the marshal of France.

"I have often noticed how ready these casks, overflowing with wit, are to open their sluices while being transported by diligence or 'bus, or by any vehicle drawn by horses, for nobody talks in a railway car.

"At the rate of our exit from Paris, the journey would take full seven hours: so I got an old corporal to talk, for my diversion. He could neither read nor write: he was entirely illiterate. Yet the journey seemed short. The corporal had been through all the campaigns, he told me of things perfectly unheard of, that historians never trouble themselves about.

"Ah! Hector, how superior is practice to theory! Among other things, and in reply to a question relative to the infantry, whose courage is much more tried by marching than by fighting, he said this, which I give you free from circumlocution:

"'Sir, when Parisians were brought to our 45th, which Napoleon called The Terrible (I am speaking of the early days of the Empire, when the infantry had legs of steel, and when they needed them), I had a way of telling beforehand which of them would remain in the 45th. They marched without hurrying, they did their little six leagues a day, neither more nor less, and they pitched camp in condition to begin again on the morrow. The plucky fellows who did ten leagues and wanted to run to the victory, stopped half way at the hospital.'

"The worthy corporal was talking of marriage while he thought he was talking of war, and you have stopped half way, Hector, at the hospital.

"Remember the sympathetic condolence of Madame de Sevigne counting out three hundred thousand francs to Monsieur de Grignan, to induce him to marry one of the prettiest girls in France! 'Why,' said she to herself, 'he will have to marry her every day, as long as she lives! Decidedly, I don't think three hundred francs too much.' Is it not enough to make the bravest tremble?

"My dear fellow, conjugal happiness is founded, like that of nations, upon ignorance. It is a felicity full of negative conditions.

"If I am happy with my little Caroline, it is due to the strictest observance of that salutary principle so strongly insisted upon in the *Physiology of Marriage*. I have resolved to lead my wife through paths beaten in the snow, until the happy day when infidelity will be difficult.

"In the situation in which you have placed yourself, and which resembles that of Duprez, who, on his first appearance at Paris, went to singing with all the voice his lungs would yield, instead of imitating Nourrit, who gave the audience just enough to enchant them, the following, I think, is your proper course to—"

The letter broke off here: Caroline returned it to its place, at the same time wondering how she would make her dear Adolphe expiate his obedience to the execrable precepts of the *Physiology of Marriage*.

A TRUCE.

This trouble doubtless occurs sufficiently often and in different ways enough in the existence of married women, for this personal incident to become the type of the genus.

The Caroline in question here is very pious, she loves her husband very much, her husband asserts that she loves him too much, even: but this is a piece of marital conceit, if, indeed, it is not a provocation, as he only complains to his wife's young lady friends.

When a person's conscience is involved, the least thing becomes exceedingly serious. Madame de — has told her young friend, Madame de Fischtaminel, that she had been compelled to make an extraordinary confession to her spiritual director, and to perform penance, the director having decided that she was in a state of mortal sin. This lady, who goes to mass every morning, is a woman of thirty-six years, thin and slightly pimpled. She has large soft black eyes, her upper lip is strongly shaded: still her voice is sweet, her manners gentle, her gait noble—she is a woman of quality.

Madame de Fischtaminel, whom Madame de — has made her friend (nearly all pious women patronize a woman who is considered worldly, on the pretext of converting her),—Madame de Fischtaminel asserts that these qualities, in this Caroline of the Pious Sort, are a victory of religion over a rather violent natural temper.

These details are necessary to describe the trouble in all its horror.

This lady's Adolphe had been compelled to leave his wife for two months, in April, immediately after the forty days' fast that Caroline scrupulously observes. Early in June, therefore, madame expected her husband, she expected him day by day. From one hope to another,

"Conceived every morn and deferred every eve."

She got along as far as Sunday, the day when her presentiments, which had now reached a state of paroxysm, told her that the longed-for husband would arrive at an early hour.

When a pious woman expects her husband, and that husband has been absent from home nearly four months, she takes much more pains with her toilet than a young girl does, though waiting for her first betrothed.

This virtuous Caroline was so completely absorbed in exclusively personal preparations, that she forgot to go to eight o'clock mass. She proposed to hear a low mass, but she was afraid of losing the delight of her dear Adolphe's first glance, in case he arrived at early dawn. Her chambermaid—who respectfully left her mistress alone in the dressing-room where pious and pimpled ladies let no one enter, not even their husbands, especially if they are thin—her chambermaid heard her exclaim several times, "If it's your master, let me know!"

The rumbling of a vehicle having made the furniture rattle, Caroline assumed a mild tone to conceal the violence of her legitimate emotions.

"Oh! 'tis he! Run, Justine: tell him I am waiting for him here." Caroline trembled so that she dropped into an arm-chair.

The vehicle was a butcher's wagon.

It was in anxieties like this that the eight o'clock mass slipped by, like an eel in his slime. Madame's toilet operations were resumed, for she was engaged in dressing. The chambermaid's nose had already been the recipient of a superb muslin chemise, with a simple hem, which Caroline had thrown at her from the dressing-room, though she had given her the same kind for the last three months.

"What are you thinking of, Justine? I told you to choose from the chemises that are not numbered."

The unnumbered chemises were only seven or eight, in the most magnificent trousseau. They are chemises gotten up and embroidered with the greatest care: a woman must be a queen, a young queen, to have a dozen. Each one of Caroline's was trimmed with valenciennes round the bottom, and still more coquettishly garnished about the neck. This feature of our manners will perhaps serve to suggest a suspicion, in the masculine world, of the domestic drama revealed by this exceptional chemise.

Petty Troubles of Married Life

Caroline had put on a pair of Scotch thread stockings, little prunella buskins, and her most deceptive corsets. She had her hair dressed in the fashion that most became her, and embellished it with a cap of the most elegant form. It is unnecessary to speak of her morning gown. A pious lady who lives at Paris and who loves her husband, knows as well as a coquette how to choose those pretty little striped patterns, have them cut with an open waist, and fastened by loops to buttons in a way which compels her to refasten them two or three times in an hour, with little airs more or less charming, as the case may be.

The nine o'clock mass, the ten o'clock mass, every mass, went by in these preparations, which, for women in love, are one of their twelve labors of Hercules.

Pious women rarely go to church in a carriage, and they are right. Except in the case of a pouring shower, or intolerably bad weather, a person ought not to appear haughty in the place where it is becoming to be humble. Caroline was afraid to compromise the freshness of her dress and the purity of her thread stockings. Alas! these pretexts concealed a reason.

"If I am at church when Adolphe comes, I shall lose the pleasure of his first glance: and he will think I prefer high mass to him."

She made this sacrifice to her husband in a desire to please him—a fearfully worldly consideration. Prefer the creature to the Creator! A husband to heaven! Go and hear a sermon and you will learn what such an offence will cost you.

"After all," says Caroline, quoting her confessor, "society is founded upon marriage, which the Church has included among its sacraments."

And this is the way in which religious instruction may be put aside in favor of a blind though legitimate love. Madame refused breakfast, and ordered the meal to be kept hot, just as she kept herself ready, at a moment's notice, to welcome the precious absentee.

Now these little things may easily excite a laugh: but in the first place they are continually occurring with couples who love each other, or where one of them loves the other: besides, in a woman so

137

strait-laced, so reserved, so worthy, as this lady, these acknowledgments of affection went beyond the limits imposed upon her feelings by the lofty self-respect which true piety induces. When Madame de Fischtaminel narrated this little scene in a devotee's life, dressing it up with choice by-play, acted out as ladies of the world know how to act out their anecdotes, I took the liberty of saying that it was the Canticle of canticles in action.

"If her husband doesn't come," said Justine to the cook, "what will become of us? She has already thrown her chemise in my face."

At last, Caroline heard the crack of a postilion's whip, the well-known rumbling of a traveling carriage, the racket made by the hoofs of post-horses, and the jingling of their bells! Oh, she could doubt no longer, the bells made her burst forth, as thus:

"The door! Open the door! 'Tis he, my husband! Will you never go to the door!" And the pious woman stamped her foot and broke the bell-rope.

"Why, madame," said Justine, with the vivacity of a servant doing her duty, "it's some people going away."

"Upon my word," replied Caroline, half ashamed, to herself, "I will never let Adolphe go traveling again without me."

A Marseilles poet—it is not known whether it was Mery or Barthelemy —acknowledged that if his best fried did not arrive punctually at the dinner hour, he waited patiently five minutes: at the tenth minute, he felt a desire to throw the napkin in his face: at the twelfth he hoped some great calamity would befall him: at the fifteenth, he would not be able to restrain himself from stabbing him several times with a dirk.

All women, when expecting somebody, are Marseilles poets, if, indeed, we may compare the vulgar throes of hunger to the sublime Canticle of canticles of a pious wife, who is hoping for the joys of a husband's first glance after a three months' absence. Let all those who love and who have met again after an absence ten thousand times accursed, be good enough to recall their first glance: it says so many things that the lovers, if in the presence of a third party, are fain to lower their eyes! This poem, in which every man is as great as Homer, in which he seems a god to the woman who loves him, is, for a pious, thin and pimpled lady, all the more immense, from the fact that she has not, like Madame de Fischtaminel, the resource of having several copies of it. In her case, her husband is all she's got!

So you will not be surprised to learn that Caroline missed every mass and had no breakfast. This hunger and thirst for Adolphe gave her a violent cramp in the stomach. She did not think of religion once during the hours of mass, nor during those of vespers. She was not comfortable when she sat, and she was very uncomfortable when she stood: Justine advised her to go to bed. Caroline, quite overcome, retired at about half past five in the evening, after having taken a light soup: but she ordered a dainty supper at ten.

"I shall doubtless sup with my husband," she said.

This speech was the conclusion of dreadful catalinics, internally fulminated. She had reached the Marseilles poet's several stabs with a dirk. So she spoke in a tone that was really terrible. At three in the morning Caroline was in a profound sleep: Adolphe arrived without her hearing either carriage, or horse, or bell, or opening door!

Adolphe, who would not permit her to be disturbed, went to bed in the spare room. When Caroline heard of his return in the morning, two tears issued from her eyes; she rushed to the spare room without the slightest preparatory toilet; a hideous attendant, posted on the threshold, informed her that her husband, having traveled two hundred leagues and been two nights without sleep, requested that he might not be awakened: he was exceedingly tired.

Caroline—pious woman that she was—opened the door violently without being able to wake the only husband that heaven had given her, and then hastened to church to listen to a thanksgiving mass.

As she was visibly snappish for three whole days, Justine remarked, in reply to an unjust reproach, and with a chambermaid's finesse:

"Why, madame, your husband's got back!"

"He has only got back to Paris," returned the pious Caroline.

USELESS CARE.

Put yourself in the place of a poor woman of doubtful beauty, who owes her husband to the weight of her dowry, who gives herself infinite pains, and spends a great deal of money to appear to advantage and follow the fashions, who does her best to keep house sumptuously and yet economically—a house, too, not easy to manage—who, from morality and dire necessity, perhaps, loves no one but her husband, who has no other study but the happiness of this precious husband, who, to express all in one word, joins the maternal sentiment *to the sentiment of her duties*. This underlined circumlocution is the paraphrase of the word love in the language of prudes.

Have you put yourself in her place? Well, this too-much-loved husband by chance remarked at his friend Monsieur de Fischtaminel's, that he was very fond of mushrooms *a l'Italienne*.

If you have paid some attention to the female nature, in its good, great, and grand manifestations, you know that for a loving wife there is no greater pleasure than that of seeing the beloved one absorbing his favorite viands. This springs from the fundamental idea upon which the affection of women is based: that of being the source of all his pleasures, big and little. Love animates everything in life, and conjugal love has a peculiar right to descend to the most trivial details.

Caroline spends two or three days in inquiries before she learns how the Italians dress mushrooms. She discovers a Corsican abbe who tells her that at Biffi's, in the rue de Richelieu, she will not only learn how the Italians dress mushrooms, but that she will be able to obtain some Milanese mushrooms. Our pious Caroline thanks the Abbe Serpolini, and resolves to send him a breviary in acknowledgment.

Caroline's cook goes to Biffi's, comes back from Biffi's, and exhibits to the countess a quantity of mushrooms as big as the coachman's ears.

"Very good," she says, "did he explain to you how to cook them?"

"Oh, for us cooks, them's a mere nothing," replies the cook.

Petty Troubles of Married Life

As a general rule, cooks know everything, in the cooking way, except how a cook may feather his nest.

At evening, during the second course, all Caroline's fibres quiver with pleasure at observing the servant bringing to the table a certain suggestive dish. She has positively waited for this dinner as she had waited for her husband.

But between waiting with certainty and expecting a positive pleasure, there is, to the souls of the elect—and everybody will include a woman who adores her husband among the elect—there is, between these two worlds of expectation, the difference that exists between a fine night and a fine day.

The dish is presented to the beloved Adolphe, he carelessly plunges his spoon in and helps himself, without perceiving Caroline's extreme emotion, to several of those soft, fat, round things, that travelers who visit Milan do not for a long time recognize; they take them for some kind of shell-fish.

"Well, Adolphe?"

"Well, dear."

"Don't you recognize them?"

"Recognize what?"

"Your mushrooms *a l'Italienne*?"

"These mushrooms! I thought they were—well, yes, they *are* mushrooms!"

"Yes, and *a l'Italienne*, too."

"Pooh, they are old preserved mushrooms, *a la milanaise*. I abominate them!"

"What kind is it you like, then?"

"*Fungi trifolati.*"

Let us observe—to the disgrace of an epoch which numbers and labels everything, which puts the whole creation in bottles, which is at this moment classifying one hundred and fifty thousand species of insects, giving them all the termination *us*, so that a *Silbermanus* is the same individual in all countries for the learned men who dissect a butterfly's legs with pincers—that we still want a nomenclature for the chemistry of the kitchen, to enable all the cooks in the world to produce precisely similar dishes. It would be diplomatically agreed that French should be the language of the kitchen, as Latin has been adopted by the scientific for botany and entomology, unless it were desired to imitate them in that, too, and thus really have kitchen Latin.

"My dear," resumes Adolphe, on seeing the clouded and lengthened face of his chaste Caroline, "in France the dish in question is called Mushrooms *a l'Italienne*, *a la provencale*, *a la bordelaise*. The mushrooms are minced, fried in oil with a few ingredients whose names I have forgotten. You add a taste of garlic, I believe—"

Talk about calamities, of petty troubles! This, do you see, is, to a woman's heart, what the pain of an extracted tooth is to a child of eight. *Ab uno disce omnes*: which means, "There's one of them: find the rest in your memory." For we have taken this culinary description as a prototype of the vexations which afflict loving but indifferently loved women.

SMOKE WITHOUT FIRE.

A woman full of faith in the man she loves is a romancer's fancy. This feminine personage no more exists than does a rich dowry. A woman's confidence glows perhaps for a few moments, at the dawn of love, and disappears in a trice like a shooting star.

With women who are neither Dutch, nor English, nor Belgian, nor from any marshy country, love is a pretext for suffering, an employment for the superabundant powers of their imaginations and their nerves.

Thus the second idea that takes possession of a happy woman, one who is really loved, is the fear of losing her happiness, for we must do her the justice to say that her first idea is to enjoy it. All who possess treasures are in dread of thieves, but they do not, like women, lend wings and feet to their golden stores.

The little blue flower of perfect felicity is not so common, that the heaven-blessed man who possesses it, should be simpleton enough to abandon it.

Axiom. — A woman is never deserted without a reason.

This axiom is written in the heart of hearts of every woman. Hence the rage of a woman deserted.

Let us not infringe upon the petty troubles of love: we live in a calculating epoch when women are seldom abandoned, do what they may: for, of all wives or women, nowadays, the legitimate is the least expensive. Now, every woman who is loved, has gone through the petty annoyance of suspicion. This suspicion, whether just or unjust, engenders a multitude of domestic troubles, and here is the biggest of all.

Caroline is one day led to notice that her cherished Adolphe leaves her rather too often upon a matter of business, that eternal Chaumontel's affair, which never comes to an end.

Axiom. — Every household has its Chaumontel's affair. (See TROUBLE WITHIN TROUBLE.)

In the first place, a woman no more believes in matters of business than publishers and managers do in the illness of actresses and authors. The moment a beloved creature absents himself, though she has rendered him even too happy, every woman straightway imagines that he has hurried away to some easy conquest. In this respect, women endow men with superhuman faculties. Fear magnifies everything, it dilates the eyes and the heart: it makes a woman mad.

"Where is my husband going? What is my husband doing? Why has he left me? Why did he not take me with him?"

These four questions are the four cardinal points of the compass of suspicion, and govern the stormy sea of soliloquies. From these frightful tempests which ravage a woman's heart springs an ignoble, unworthy resolution, one which every woman, the duchess as well as the shopkeeper's wife, the baroness as well as the stockbroker's lady, the angel as well as the shrew, the indifferent as well as the passionate, at once puts into execution. They imitate the government, every one of them; they resort to espionage. What the State has invented in the public interest, they consider legal, legitimate and permissible, in the interest of their love. This fatal woman's curiosity reduces them to the necessity of having agents, and the agent of any woman who, in this situation, has not lost her self-respect,—a situation in which her jealousy will not permit her to respect anything: neither your little boxes, nor your clothes, nor the drawers of your treasury, of your desk, of your table, of your bureau, nor your pocketbook with private compartments, nor your papers, nor your traveling dressing-case, nor your toilet articles (a woman discovers in this way that her husband dyed his moustache when he was a bachelor), nor your india-rubber girdles—her agent, I say, the only one in whom a woman trusts, is her maid, for her maid understands her, excuses her, and approves her.

In the paroxysm of excited curiosity, passion and jealousy, a woman makes no calculations, takes no observations. She simply wishes to know the whole truth.

And Justine is delighted: she sees her mistress compromising herself with her, and she espouses her passion, her dread, her fears and her suspicions, with terrible friendship. Justine and Caroline hold councils and have secret interviews. All espionage involves such relationships. In this pass, a maid becomes the arbitress of the fate of the married couple. Example: Lord Byron.

"Madame," Justine one day observes, "monsieur really *does* go out to see a woman."

Caroline turns pale.

"But don't be alarmed, madame, it's an old woman."

"Ah, Justine, to some men no women are old: men are inexplicable."

"But, madame, it isn't a lady, it's a woman, quite a common woman."

"Ah, Justine, Lord Byron loved a fish-wife at Venice, Madame de Fischtaminel told me so."

And Caroline bursts into tears.

"I've been pumping Benoit."

"What is Benoit's opinion?"

"Benoit thinks that the woman is a go-between, for monsieur keeps his secret from everybody, even from Benoit."

For a week Caroline lives the life of the damned; all her savings go to pay spies and to purchase reports.

Finally, Justine goes to see the woman, whose name is Madame Mahuchet; she bribes her and learns at last that her master has preserved a witness of his youthful follies, a nice little boy that looks very much like him, and that this woman is his nurse, the second-hand mother who has charge of little Frederick, who pays his quarterly school-bills, and through whose hands pass the twelve hundred or two thousand francs which Adolphe is supposed annually to lose at cards.

"What of the mother?" exclaims Caroline.

To end the matter, Justine, Caroline's good genius, proves to her that M'lle Suzanne Beauminet, formerly a grisette and somewhat later

Madame Sainte-Suzanne, died at the hospital, or else that she has made her fortune, or else, again, that her place in society is so low there is no danger of madame's ever meeting her.

Caroline breathes again: the dirk has been drawn from her heart, she is quite happy; but she had no children but daughters, and would like a boy. This little drama of unjust suspicions, this comedy of the conjectures to which Mother Mahuchet gives rise, these phases of a causeless jealousy, are laid down here as the type of a situation, the varieties of which are as innumerable as characters, grades and sorts.

This source of petty troubles is pointed out here, in order that women seated upon the river's bank may contemplate in it the course of their own married life, following its ascent or descent, recalling their own adventures to mind, their untold disasters, the foibles which caused their errors, and the peculiar fatalities to which were due an instant of frenzy, a moment of unnecessary despair, or sufferings which they might have spared themselves, happy in their self-delusions.

This vexation has a corollary in the following, one which is much more serious and often without remedy, especially when its root lies among vices of another kind, and which do not concern us, for, in this work, women are invariably esteemed honest—until the end.

THE DOMESTIC TYRANT.

"My dear Caroline," says Adolphe one day to his wife, "are you satisfied with Justine?"

"Yes, dear, quite so."

"Don't you think she speaks to you rather impertinently?"

"Do you suppose I would notice a maid? But it seems *you* notice her!"

"What do you say?" asks Adolphe in an indignant way that is always delightful to women.

Justine is a genuine maid for an actress, a woman of thirty stamped by the small-pox with innumerable dimples, in which the loves are far from sporting: she is as brown as opium, has a good deal of leg and not much body, gummy eyes, and a tournure to match. She would like to have Benoit marry her, but at this unexpected suggestion, Benoit asked for his discharge. Such is the portrait of the domestic tyrant enthroned by Caroline's jealousy.

Justine takes her coffee in the morning, in bed, and manages to have it as good as, not to say better than, that of her mistress. Justine sometimes goes out without asking leave, dressed like the wife of a second-class banker. She sports a pink hat, one of her mistress' old gowns made over, an elegant shawl, shoes of bronze kid, and jewelry of doubtful character.

Justine is sometimes in a bad humor, and makes her mistress feel that she too is a woman like herself, though she is not married. She has her whims, her fits of melancholy, her caprices. She even dares to have her nerves! She replies curtly, she makes herself insupportable to the other servants, and, to conclude, her wages have been considerably increased.

"My dear, this girl is getting more intolerable every day," says Adolphe one morning to his wife, on noticing Justine listening at the key-hole, "and if you don't send her away, I will!"

Caroline, greatly alarmed, is obliged to give Justine a talking to, while her husband is out.

"Justine, you take advantage of my kindness to you: you have high wages, here, you have perquisites, presents: try to keep your place, for my husband wants to send you away."

The maid humbles herself to the earth, she sheds tears: she is so attached to madame! Ah! she would rush into the fire for her: she would let herself be chopped into mince-meat: she is ready for anything.

"If you had anything to conceal, madame, I would take it on myself and say it was me!"

"Very well, Justine, very good, my girl," says Caroline, terrified: "but that's not the point: just try to keep in your place."

"Ah, ha!" says Justine to herself, "monsieur wants to send me away, does he? Wait and see the deuce of a life I'll lead you, you old curmudgeon!"

A week after, Justine, who is dressing her mistress' hair, looks in the glass to make sure that Caroline can see all the grimaces of her countenance: and Caroline very soon inquires, "Why, what's the matter, Justine?"

"I would tell you, readily, madame, but then, madame, you are so weak with monsieur!"

"Come, go on, what is it?"

"I know now, madame, why master wanted to show me the door: he has confidence in nobody but Benoit, and Benoit is playing the mum with me."

"Well, what does that prove? Has anything been discovered?"

"I'm sure that between the two they are plotting something against you madame," returns the maid with authority.

Caroline, whom Justine watches in the glass, turns pale: all the tortures of the previous petty trouble return, and Justine sees that

148

she has become as indispensable to her mistress as spies are to the government when a conspiracy is discovered. Still, Caroline's friends do not understand why she keeps so disagreeable a servant girl, one who wears a hat, whose manners are impertinent, and who gives herself the airs of a lady.

This stupid domination is talked of at Madame Deschars', at Madame de Fischtaminel's, and the company consider it funny. A few ladies think they can see certain monstrous reasons for it, reasons which compromise Caroline's honor.

Axiom.—In society, people can put cloaks on every kind of truth, even the prettiest.

In short the *aria della calumnia* is executed precisely as if Bartholo were singing it.

It is averred that Caroline cannot discharge her maid.

Society devotes itself desperately to discovering the secret of this enigma. Madame de Fischtaminel makes fun of Adolphe who goes home in a rage, has a scene with Caroline and discharges Justine.

This produces such an effect upon Justine, that she falls sick, and takes to her bed. Caroline observes to her husband, that it would be awkward to turn a girl in Justine's condition into the street, a girl who is so much attached to them, too, and who has been with them sine their marriage.

"Let her go then as soon as she is well!" says Adolphe.

Caroline, reassured in regard to Adolphe, and indecently swindled by Justine, at last comes to desire to get rid of her: she applies a violent remedy to the disease, and makes up her mind to go under the Caudine Forks of another petty trouble, as follows:

THE AVOWAL.

One morning, Adolphe is petted in a very unusual manner. The too happy husband wonders what may be the cause of this development of affection, and he hears Caroline, in her most winning tones, utter the word: "Adolphe?"

"Well?" he replies, in alarm at the internal agitation betrayed by Caroline's voice.

"Promise not to be angry."

"Well."

"Not to be vexed with me."

"Never. Go on."

"To forgive me and never say anything about it."

"But tell me what it is!"

"Besides, you are the one that's in the wrong—"

"Speak, or I'll go away."

"There's no one but you that can get me out of the scrape—and it was you that got me into it."

"Come, come."

"It's about—"

"About—"

"About Justine!"

"Don't speak of her, she's discharged. I won't see her again, her style of conduct exposes your reputation—"

"What can people say—what have they said?"

The scene changes, the result of which is a secondary explanation which makes Caroline blush, as she sees the bearing of the suppositions of her best friends.

"Well, now, Adolphe, it's to you I owe all this. Why didn't you tell me about Frederick?"

"Frederick the Great? The King of Prussia?"

"What creatures men are! Hypocrite, do you want to make me believe that you have forgotten your son so soon, M'lle Suzanne Beauminet's son?"

"Then you know—?"

"The whole thing! And old other Mahuchet, and your absences from home to give him a good dinner on holidays."

"How like moles you pious women can be if you try!" exclaims Adolphe, in his terror.

"It was Justine that found it out."

"Ah! Now I understand the reason of her insolence."

"Oh, your Caroline has been very wretched, dear, and this spying system, which was produced by my love for you, for I do love you, and madly too,—if you deceived me, I would fly to the extremity of creation,—well, as I was going to say, this unfounded jealousy has put me in Justine's power, so, my precious, get me out of it the best way you can!"

"Let this teach you, my angel, never to make use of your servants, if you want them to be of use to you. It is the lowest of tyrannies, this being at the mercy of one's people."

Adolphe takes advantage of this circumstance to alarm Caroline, he thinks of future Chaumontel's affairs, and would be glad to have no more espionage.

Justine is sent for, Adolphe peremptorily dismisses her without waiting to hear her explanation. Caroline imagines her vexations at an end. She gets another maid.

Justine, whose twelve or fifteen thousand francs have attracted the notice of a water carrier, becomes Madame Chavagnac, and goes into the apple business. Ten months after, in Adolphe's absence, Caroline receives a letter written upon school-boy paper, in strides which would require orthopedic treatment for three months, and thus conceived:

"Madam!

"Yu ar shaimphoolly diseeved bi yure huzban fur mame Deux fischtaminelle, hee goze their evry eavning, yu ar az blynde az a Batt. Your gott wott yu dizzurv, and I am Glad ovit, and I have thee honur ov prezenting yu the assurunz ov Mi moaste ds Sting guischt respecks."

Caroline starts like a lion who has been stung by a bumble-bee; she places herself once more, and of her own accord, upon the griddle of suspicion, and begins her struggle with the unknown all over again.

When she has discovered the injustice of her suspicions, there comes another letter with an offer to furnish her with details relative to a Chaumontel's affair which Justine has unearthed.

The petty trouble of avowals, ladies, is often more serious than this, as you perhaps have occasion to remember.

HUMILIATIONS.

To the glory of women, let it be said, they care for their husbands even when their husbands care no more for them, not only because there are more ties, socially speaking, between a married woman and a man, than between the man and the wife; but also because woman has more delicacy and honor than man, the chief conjugal question apart, as a matter of course.

Axiom.—In a husband, there is only a man; in a married woman, there is a man, a father, a mother and a woman.

A married woman has sensibility enough for four, or for five even, if you look closely.

Now, it is not improper to observe in this place, that, in a woman's eyes, love is a general absolution: the man who is a good lover may commit crimes, if he will, he is always as pure as snow in the eyes of her who loves him, if he truly loves her. As to a married woman, loved or not, she feels so deeply that the honor and consideration of her husband are the fortune of her children, that she acts like the woman in love,—so active is the sense of community of interest.

This profound sentiment engenders, for certain Carolines, petty troubles which, unfortunately for this book, have their dismal side.

Adolphe is compromised. We will not enumerate all the methods of compromising oneself, for we might become personal. Let us take, as an example, the social error which our epoch excuses, permits, understands and commits the most of any—the case of an honest robbery, of skillfully concealed corruption in office, or of some misrepresentation that becomes excusable when it has succeeded, as, for instance, having an understanding with parties in power, for the sale of property at the highest possible price to a city, or a country.

Thus, in a bankruptcy, Adolphe, in order to protect himself (this means to recover his claims), has become mixed up in certain unlawful doings which may bring a man to the necessity of testifying before the Court of Assizes. In fact, it is not known that the daring creditor will not be considered a party.

Take notice that in all cases of bankruptcy, protecting oneself is regarded as the most sacred of duties, even by the most respectable houses: the thing is to keep the bad side of the protection out of sight, as they do in prudish England.

Adolphe does not know what to do, as his counsel has told him not to appear in the matter: so he has recourse to Caroline. He gives her a lesson, he coaches her, he teaches her the Code, he examines her dress, he equips her as a brig sent on a voyage, and despatches her to the office of some judge, or some syndic. The judge is apparently a man of severe morality, but in reality a libertine: he retains his serious expression on seeing a pretty woman enter, and makes sundry very uncomplimentary remarks about Adolphe.

"I pity you, madame, you belong to a man who may involve you in numerous unpleasant affairs: a few more matters like this, and he will be quite disgraced. Have you any children? Excuse my asking; you are so young, it is perfectly natural." And the judge comes as near to Caroline as possible.

"Yes, sir."

"Ah, great heavens! what a prospect is yours! My first thought was for the woman, but now I pity you doubly, I think of the mother. Ah, how you must have suffered in coming here! Poor, poor woman!"

"Ah, sir, you take an interest in me, do you not?"

"Alas, what can I do?" says the judge, darting a glance sidewise at Caroline. "What you ask of me is a dereliction of duty, and I am a magistrate before I am a man."

"Oh, sir, only be a man—"

"Are you aware of the full bearing of that request, fair creature?" At this point the magistrate tremblingly takes Caroline's hand.

Caroline, who remembers that the honor of her husband and children is at stake, says to herself that this is not the time to play the prude. She abandons her hand, making just resistance enough for the old man (happily he is an old man) to consider it a favor.

"Come, come, my beauty," resumes the judge, "I should be loath to cause so lovely a woman to shed tears; we'll see about it. You shall come to-morrow evening and tell me the whole affair. We must look at the papers, we will examine them together—"

"Sir—"

"It's indispensable."

"But, sir—"

"Don't be alarmed, my dear, a judge is likely to know how to grant what is due to justice and—" he puts on a shrewd look here—"to beauty."

"But, sir—"

"Be quite at your ease," he adds, holding her hand closely in his, "and we'll try to reduce this great crime down to a peccadillo." And he goes to the door with Caroline, who is frightened to death at an appointment thus proposed.

The syndic is a lively young man, and he receives Madame Adolphe with a smile. He smiles at everything, and he smiles as he takes her round the waist with an agility which leaves Caroline no time to resist, especially as she says to herself, "Adolphe particularly recommended me not to vex the syndic."

Nevertheless Caroline escapes, in the interest of the syndic himself, and again pronounces the "Sir!" which she had said three times to the judge.

"Don't be angry with me, you are irresistible, you are an angel, and your husband is a monster: for what does he mean by sending a siren to a young man whom he knows to be inflammable!"

"Sir, my husband could not come himself; he is in bed, very sick, and you threatened him so terribly that the urgency of the matter—"

"Hasn't he got a lawyer, an attorney?"

Caroline is terrified by this remark which reveals Adolphe's profound rascality.

"He supposed, sir, that you would have pity upon the mother of a family, upon her children—"

"Ta, ta, ta," returns the syndic. "You have come to influence my independence, my conscience, you want me to give the creditors up to you: well, I'll do more, I give you up my heart, my fortune! Your husband wants to save *his* honor, *my* honor is at your disposal!"

"Sir," cries Caroline, as she tries to raise the syndic who has thrown himself at her feet. "You alarm me!"

She plays the terrified female and thus reaches the door, getting out of a delicate situation as women know how to do it, that is, without compromising anything or anybody.

"I will come again," she says smiling, "when you behave better."

"You leave me thus! Take care! Your husband may yet find himself seated at the bar of the Court of Assizes: he is accessory to a fraudulent bankruptcy, and we know several things about him that are not by any means honorable. It is not his first departure from rectitude; he has done a good many dirty things, he has been mixed up in disgraceful intrigues, and you are singularly careful of the honor of a man who cares as little for his own honor as he does for yours."

Caroline, alarmed by these words, lets go the door, shuts it and comes back.

"What do you mean, sir?" she exclaims, furious at this outrageous broadside.

"Why, this affair—"

"Chaumontel's affair?"

"No, his speculations in houses that he had built by people that were insolvent."

Caroline remembers the enterprise undertaken by Adolphe to double his income: (See *The Jesuitism of Women*) she trembles. Her curiosity is in the syndic's favor.

156

"Sit down here. There, at this distance, I will behave well, but I can look at you."

And he narrates, at length, the conception due to du Tillet the banker, interrupting himself to say: "Oh, what a pretty, cunning, little foot; no one but you could have such a foot as that—*Du Tillet, therefore, compromised.* What an ear, too! You have been doubtless told that you had a delicious ear—*And du Tillet was right, for judgment had already been given*—I love small ears, but let me have a model of yours, and I will do anything you like—*du Tillet profited by this to throw the whole loss on your idiotic husband*: oh, what a charming silk, you are divinely dressed!"

"Where were we, sir?"

"How can I remember while admiring your Raphaelistic head?"

At the twenty-seventh compliment, Caroline considers the syndic a man of wit: she makes him a polite speech, and goes away without learning much more of the enterprise which, not long before had swallowed up three hundred thousand francs.

There are many huge variations of this petty trouble.

EXAMPLE. Adolphe is brave and susceptible: he is walking on the Champs Elysees, where there is a crowd of people; in this crowd are several ill-mannered young men who indulge in jokes of doubtful propriety: Caroline puts up with them and pretends not to hear them, in order to keep her husband out of a duel.

ANOTHER EXAMPLE. A child belonging to the genus Terrible, exclaims in the presence of everybody:

"Mamma, would you let Justine hit me?"

"Certainly not."

"Why do you ask, my little man?" inquires Madame Foullepointe.

"Because she just gave father a big slap, and he's ever so much stronger than me."

Madame Foullepointe laughs, and Adolphe, who intended to pay court to her, is cruelly joked by her, after having had a first last quarrel with Caroline.

THE LAST QUARREL.

In every household, husbands and wives must one day hear the striking of a fatal hour. It is a knell, the death and end of jealousy, a great, noble and charming passion, the only true symptom of love, if it is not even its double. When a woman is no longer jealous of her husband, all is over, she loves him no more. So, conjugal love expires in the last quarrel that a woman gives herself the trouble to raise.

Axiom.—When a woman ceases to quarrel with her husband, the Minotaur has seated himself in a corner arm-chair, tapping his boots with his cane.

Every woman must remember her last quarrel, that supreme petty trouble which often explodes about nothing, but more often still on some occasion of a brutal fact or of a decisive proof. This cruel farewell to faith, to the childishness of love, to virtue even, is in a degree as capricious as life itself. Like life it varies in every house.

Here, the author ought perhaps to search out all the varieties of quarrels, if he desires to be precise.

Thus, Caroline may have discovered that the judicial robe of the syndic in Chaumontel's affair, hides a robe of infinitely softer stuff, of an agreeable, silky color: that Chaumontel's hair, in short, is fair, and that his eyes are blue.

Or else Caroline, who arose before Adolphe, may have seen his greatcoat thrown wrong side out across a chair; the edge of a little perfumed paper, just peeping out of the side-pocket, may have attracted her by its whiteness, like a ray of the sun entering a dark room through a crack in the window: or else, while taking Adolphe in her arms and feeling his pocket, she may have caused the note to crackle: or else she may have been informed of the state of things by a foreign odor that she has long noticed upon him, and may have read these lines:

"Ungraitfull wun, wot du yu supoz I no About Hipolite. Kum, and yu shal se whether I Love yu."

Or this:

"Yesterday, love, you made me wait for you: what will it be to-morrow?"

Or this:

"The women who love you, my dear sir, are very unhappy in hating you so, when you are not with them: take care, for the hatred which exists during your absence, may possibly encroach upon the hours you spend in their company."

Or this:

"You traitorous Chodoreille, what were you doing yesterday on the boulevard with a woman hanging on your arm? If it was your wife, accept my compliments of condolence upon her absent charms: she has doubtless deposited them at the pawnbroker's, and the ticket to redeem them with is lost."

Four notes emanating from the grisette, the lady, the pretentious woman in middle life, and the actress, among whom Adolphe has chosen his *belle* (according to the Fischtaminellian vocabulary).

Or else Caroline, taken veiled by Ferdinand to Ranelagh Garden, sees with her own eyes Adolphe abandoning himself furiously to the polka, holding one of the ladies of honor to Queen Pomare in his arms; or else, again, Adolphe has for the seventh time, made a mistake in the name, and called his wife Juliette, Charlotte or Lisa: or, a grocer or restaurateur sends to the house, during Adolphe's absence, certain damning bills which fall into Caroline's hands.

PAPERS RELATING TO CHAUMONTEL'S AFFAIR.

(Private Tables Served.)

M. Adolphe to Perrault,

To 1 Pate de Foie Gras delivered at Madame Schontz's, the 6th of January,	fr. 22.50
Six bottle of assorted wines,	70.00
To one special breakfast delivered at Congress Hotel, the 11th of February, at No. 21 — Stipulated price,	100.00
Total,	Francs, 192.50

Caroline examines the dates and remembers them as appointments made for business connected with Chaumontel's affair. Adolphe had designated the sixth of January as the day fixed for a meeting at which the creditors in Chaumontel's affair were to receive the sums due them. On the eleventh of February he had an appointment with the notary, in order to sign a receipt relative to Chaumontel's affair.

Or else—but an attempt to mention all the chances of discovery would be the undertaking of a madman.

Every woman will remember to herself how the bandage with which her eyes were bound fell off: how, after many doubts, and agonies of heart, she made up her mind to have a final quarrel for the simple purpose of finishing the romance, putting the seal to the book, stipulating for her independence, or beginning life over again.

Some women are fortunate enough to have anticipated their husbands, and they then have the quarrel as a sort of justification.

Nervous women give way to a burst of passion and commit acts of violence.

Women of mild temper assume a decided tone which appalls the most intrepid husbands. Those who have no vengeance ready shed a great many tears.

Those who love you forgive you. Ah, they conceive so readily, like the woman called "Ma berline," that their Adolphe must be loved by the women of France, that they are rejoiced to possess, legally, a man about whom everybody goes crazy.

Certain women with lips tight shut like a vise, with a muddy complexion and thin arms, treat themselves to the malicious pleasure of promenading their Adolphe through the quagmire of falsehood and contradiction: they question him (see *Troubles within Troubles*), like a magistrate examining a criminal, reserving the spiteful enjoyment of crushing his denials by positive proof at a decisive moment. Generally, in this supreme scene of conjugal life, the fair sex is the executioner, while, in the contrary case, man is the assassin.

This is the way of it: This last quarrel (you shall know why the author has called it the *last*), is always terminated by a solemn, sacred promise, made by scrupulous, noble, or simply intelligent women (that is to say, by all women), and which we give here in its grandest form.

"Enough, Adolphe! We love each other no more; you have deceived me, and I shall never forget it. I may forgive it, but I can never forget it."

Women represent themselves as implacable only to render their forgiveness charming: they have anticipated God.

"We have now to live in common like two friends," continues Caroline. "Well, let us live like two comrades, two brothers, I do not wish to make your life intolerable, and I never again will speak to you of what has happened—"

Adolphe gives Caroline his hand: she takes it, and shakes it in the English style. Adolphe thanks Caroline, and catches a glimpse of bliss: he has converted his wife into a sister, and hopes to be a bachelor again.

The next day Caroline indulges in a very witty allusion (Adolphe cannot help laughing at it) to Chaumontel's affair. In society she makes general remarks which, to Adolphe, are very particular remarks, about their last quarrel.

At the end of a fortnight a day never passes without Caroline's recalling their last quarrel by saying: "It was the day when I found Chaumontel's bill in your pocket:" or "it happened since our last quarrel:" or, "it was the day when, for the first time, I had a clear idea of life," etc. She assassinates Adolphe, she martyrizes him! In society she gives utterance to terrible things.

"We are happy, my dear [to a lady], when we love each other no longer: it's then that we learn how to make ourselves beloved," and she looks at Ferdinand.

In short, the last quarrel never comes to an end, and from this fact flows the following axiom:

Axiom.—Putting yourself in the wrong with your lawful wife, is solving the problem of Perpetual Motion.

A SIGNAL FAILURE.

Women, and especially married women, stick ideas into their brain-pan precisely as they stick pins into a pincushion, and the devil himself, —do you mind?—could not get them out: they reserve to themselves the exclusive right of sticking them in, pulling them out, and sticking them in again.

Caroline is riding home one evening from Madame Foullepointe's in a violent state of jealousy and ambition.

Madame Foullepointe, the lioness—but this word requires an explanation. It is a fashionable neologism, and gives expression to certain rather meagre ideas relative to our present society: you must use it, if you want to describe a woman who is all the rage. This lioness rides on horseback every day, and Caroline has taken it into her head to learn to ride also.

Observe that in this conjugal phase, Adolphe and Caroline are in the season which we have denominated *A Household Revolution*, and that they have had two or three *Last Quarrels*.

"Adolphe," she says, "do you want to do me a favor?"

"Of course."

"Won't you refuse?"

"If your request is reasonable, I am willing—"

"Ah, already—that's a true husband's word—if—"

"Come, what is it?"

"I want to learn to ride on horseback."

"Now, is it a possible thing, Caroline?"

Caroline looks out of the window, and tries to wipe away a dry tear.

"Listen," resumes Adolphe; "I cannot let you go alone to the riding-school; and I cannot go with you while business gives me the annoyance it does now. What's the matter? I think I have given you unanswerable reasons."

Adolphe foresees the hiring of a stable, the purchase of a pony, the introduction of a groom and of a servant's horse into the establishment—in short, all the nuisance of female lionization.

When a man gives a woman reasons instead of giving her what she wants —well, few men have ventured to descend into that small abyss called the heart, to test the power of the tempest that suddenly bursts forth there.

"Reasons! If you want reasons, here they are!" exclaims Caroline. "I am your wife: you don't seem to care to please me any more. And as to the expenses, you greatly overrate them, my dear."

Women have as many inflections of voice to pronounce these words, *My dear*, as the Italians have to say *Amico*. I have counted twenty-nine which express only various degrees of hatred.

"Well, you'll see," resumes Caroline, "I shall be sick, and you will pay the apothecary and the doctor as much as the price of a horse. I shall be walled up here at home, and that's all you want. I asked the favor of you, though I was sure of a refusal: I only wanted to know how you would go to work to give it."

"But, Caroline—"

"Leave me alone at the riding-school!" she continues without listening. "Is that a reason? Can't I go with Madame de Fischtaminel? Madame de Fischtaminel is learning to ride on horseback, and I don't imagine that Monsieur de Fischtaminel goes with her."

"But, Caroline—"

"I am delighted with your solicitude. You think a great deal of me, really. Monsieur de Fischtaminel has more confidence in his wife, than you have in yours. He does not go with her, not he! Perhaps it's on account of this confidence that you don't want me at the school, where I might see your goings on with the fair Fischtaminel."

Adolphe tries to hide his vexation at this torrent of words, which begins when they are still half way from home, and has no sea to empty into. When Caroline is in her room, she goes on in the same way.

"You see that if reasons could restore my health or prevent me from desiring a kind of exercise pointed out by nature herself, I should not be in want of reasons, and that I know all the reasons that there are, and that I went over with the reasons before I spoke to you."

This, ladies, may with the more truth be called the prologue to the conjugal drama, from the fact that it is vigorously delivered, embellished with a commentary of gestures, ornamented with glances and all the other vignettes with which you usually illustrate such masterpieces.

Caroline, when she has once planted in Adolphe's heart the apprehension of a scene of constantly reiterated demands, feels her hatred for his control largely increase. Madame pouts, and she pouts so fiercely, that Adolphe is forced to notice it, on pain of very disagreeable consequences, for all is over, be sure of that, between two beings married by the mayor, or even at Gretna Green, when one of them no longer notices the sulkings of the other.

Axiom.—A sulk that has struck in is a deadly poison.

It was to prevent this suicide of love that our ingenious France invented boudoirs. Women could not well have Virgil's willows in the economy of our modern dwellings. On the downfall of oratories, these little cubbies become boudoirs.

This conjugal drama has three acts. The act of the prologue is already played. Then comes the act of false coquetry: one of those in which French women have the most success.

Adolphe is walking about the room, divesting himself of his apparel, and the man thus engaged, divests himself of his strength as well as of his clothing. To every man of forty, this axiom will appear profoundly just:

Axiom.—The ideas of a man who has taken his boots and his suspenders off, are no longer those of a man who is still sporting these two tyrants of the mind.

Take notice that this is only an axiom in wedded life. In morals, it is what we call a relative theorem.

Caroline watches, like a jockey on the race course, the moment when she can distance her adversary. She makes her preparations to be irresistibly fascinating to Adolphe.

Women possess a power of mimicking pudicity, a knowledge of secrets which might be those of a frightened dove, a particular register for singing, like Isabella, in the fourth act of *Robert le Diable:* *"Grace pour toi! Grace pour moi!"* which leave jockeys and horse trainers whole miles behind. As usual, the *Diable* succumbs. It is the eternal history, the grand Christian mystery of the bruised serpent, of the delivered woman becoming the great social force, as the Fourierists say. It is especially in this that the difference between the Oriental slave and the Occidental wife appears.

Upon the conjugal pillow, the second act ends by a number of onomatopes, all of them favorable to peace. Adolphe, precisely like children in the presence of a slice of bread and molasses, promises everything that Caroline wants.

THIRD ACT. As the curtain rises, the stage represents a chamber in a state of extreme disorder. Adolphe, in his dressing gown, tries to go out furtively and without waking Caroline, who is sleeping profoundly, and finally does go out.

Caroline, exceedingly happy, gets up, consults her mirror, and makes inquiries about breakfast. An hour afterward, when she is ready she learns that breakfast is served.

"Tell monsieur."

"Madame, he is in the little parlor."

"What a nice man he is," she says, going up to Adolphe, and talking the babyish, caressing language of the honey-moon.

"What for, pray?"

"Why, to let his little Liline ride the horsey."

OBSERVATION. During the honey-moon, some few married couples,—very young ones,—make use of languages, which, in ancient days, Aristotle classified and defined. (See his Pedagogy.) Thus they are perpetually using such terminations as *lala*, *nana*, *coachy-poachy*, just as mothers and nurses use them to babies. This is one of the secret reasons, discussed and recognized in big quartos by the Germans, which determined the Cabires, the creators of the Greek mythology, to represent Love as a child. There are other reasons very well known to women, the principal of which is, that, in their opinion, love in men is always *small*.

"Where did you get that idea, my sweet? You must have dreamed it!"

"What!"

Caroline stands stark still: she opens wide her eyes which are already considerably widened by amazement. Being inwardly epileptic, she says not a word: she merely gazes at Adolphe. Under the satanic fires of their gaze, Adolphe turns half way round toward the dining-room; but he asks himself whether it would not be well to let Caroline take one lesson, and to tip the wink to the riding-master, to disgust her with equestrianism by the harshness of his style of instruction.

There is nothing so terrible as an actress who reckons upon a success, and who *fait four*.

In the language of the stage, to *faire four* is to play to a wretchedly thin house, or to obtain not the slightest applause. It is taking great pains for nothing, in short a *signal failure*.

This petty trouble—it is very petty—is reproduced in a thousand ways in married life, when the honey-moon is over, and when the wife has no personal fortune.

In spite of the author's repugnance to inserting anecdotes in an exclusively aphoristic work, the tissue of which will bear nothing but the most delicate and subtle observations,—from the nature of the subject at least,—it seems to him necessary to illustrate this page by an incident narrated by one of our first physicians. This repetition of the subject involves a rule of conduct very much in use with the doctors of Paris.

A certain husband was in our Adolphe's situation. His Caroline, having once made a signal failure, was determined to conquer, for Caroline often does conquer! (See *The Physiology of Marriage*, Meditation XXVI, Paragraph *Nerves*.) She had been lying about on the sofas for two months, getting up at noon, taking no part in the amusements of the city. She would not go to the theatre,—oh, the disgusting atmosphere!—the lights, above all, the lights! Then the bustle, coming out, going in, the music,—it might be fatal, it's so terribly exciting!

She would not go on excursions to the country, oh, certainly it was her desire to do so!—but she would like (desiderata) a carriage of her own, horses of her own—her husband would not give her an equipage. And as to going in hacks, in hired conveyances, the bare thought gave her a rising at the stomach!

She would not have any cooking—the smell of the meats produced a sudden nausea. She drank innumerable drugs that her maid never saw her take.

In short, she expended large amounts of time and money in attitudes, privations, effects, pearl-white to give her the pallor of a corpse, machinery, and the like, precisely as when the manager of a theatre spreads rumors about a piece gotten up in a style of Oriental magnificence, without regard to expense!

This couple had got so far as to believe that even a journey to the springs, to Ems, to Hombourg, to Carlsbad, would hardly cure the invalid: but madame would not budge, unless she could go in her own carriage. Always that carriage!

Adolphe held out, and would not yield.

Caroline, who was a woman of great sagacity, admitted that her husband was right.

"Adolphe is right," she said to her friends, "it is I who am unreasonable: he can not, he ought not, have a carriage yet: men know better than we do the situation of their business."

At times Adolphe was perfectly furious! Women have ways about them that demand the justice of Tophet itself. Finally, during the third month, he met one of his school friends, a lieutenant in the corps of physicians, modest as all young doctors are: he had had his epaulettes one day only, and could give the order to fire!

"For a young woman, a young doctor," said our Adolphe to himself.

And he proposed to the future Bianchon to visit his wife and tell him the truth about her condition.

"My dear, it is time that you should have a physician," said Adolphe that evening to his wife, "and here is the best for a pretty woman."

The novice makes a conscientious examination, questions madame, feels her pulse discreetly, inquires into the slightest symptoms, and, at the end, while conversing, allows a smile, an expression, which, if not ironical, are extremely incredulous, to play involuntarily upon his lips, and his lips are quite in sympathy with his eyes. He prescribes some insignificant remedy, and insists upon its importance, promising to call again to observe its effect. In the ante-chamber, thinking himself alone with his school-mate, he indulges in an inexpressible shrug of the shoulders.

"There's nothing the matter with your wife, my boy," he says: "she is trifling with both you and me."

"Well, I thought so."

"But if she continues the joke, she will make herself sick in earnest: I am too sincerely your friend to enter into such a speculation, for I am determined that there shall be an honest man beneath the physician, in me—"

"My wife wants a carriage."

As in the *Solo on the Hearse*, this Caroline listened at the door.

Even at the present day, the young doctor is obliged to clear his path of the calumnies which this charming woman is continually throwing into it: and for the sake of a quiet life, he has been obliged to confess his little error—a young man's error—and to mention his enemy by name, in order to close her lips.

THE CHESTNUTS IN THE FIRE.

No one can tell how many shades and gradations there are in misfortune, for everything depends upon the character of the individual, upon the force of the imagination, upon the strength of the nerves. If it is impossible to catch these so variable shades, we may at least point out the most striking colors, and the principal attendant incidents. The author has therefore reserved this petty trouble for the last, for it is the only one that is at once comic and disastrous.

The author flatters himself that he has mentioned the principal examples. Thus, women who have arrived safely at the haven, the happy age of forty, the period when they are delivered from scandal, calumny, suspicion, when their liberty begins: these women will certainly do him the justice to state that all the critical situations of a family are pointed out or represented in this book.

Caroline has her Chaumontel's affair. She has learned how to induce Adolphe to go out unexpectedly, and has an understanding with Madame de Fischtaminel.

In every household, within a given time, ladies like Madame de Fischtaminel become Caroline's main resource.

Caroline pets Madame de Fischtaminel with all the tenderness that the African army is now bestowing upon Abd-el-Kader: she is as solicitous in her behalf as a physician is anxious to avoid curing a rich hypochondriac. Between the two, Caroline and Madame de Fischtaminel invent occupations for dear Adolphe, when neither of them desire the presence of that demigod among their penates. Madame de Fischtaminel and Caroline, who have become, through the efforts of Madame Foullepointe, the best friends in the world, have even gone so far as to learn and employ that feminine free-masonry, the rites of which cannot be made familiar by any possible initiation.

If Caroline writes the following little note to Madame de Fischtaminel:

"Dearest Angel:

"You will probably see Adolphe to-morrow, but do not keep him too long, for I want to go to ride with him at five: but if you are desirous of taking him to ride yourself, do so and I will take him up. You ought to teach me your secret for entertaining used-up people as you do."

Madame de Fischtaminel says to herself: "Gracious! So I shall have that fellow on my hands to-morrow from twelve o'clock to five."

Axiom.—Men do not always know a woman's positive request when they see it; but another woman never mistakes it: she does the contrary.

Those sweet little beings called women, and especially Parisian women, are the prettiest jewels that social industry has invented. Those who do not adore them, those who do not feel a constant jubilation at seeing them laying their plots while braiding their hair, creating special idioms for themselves and constructing with their slender fingers machines strong enough to destroy the most powerful fortunes, must be wanting in a positive sense.

On one occasion Caroline takes the most minute precautions. She writes the day before to Madame Foullepointe to go to St. Maur with Adolphe, to look at a piece of property for sale there. Adolphe would go to breakfast with her. She aids Adolphe in dressing. She twits him with the care he bestows upon his toilet, and asks absurd questions about Madame Foullepointe.

"She's real nice, and I think she is quite tired of Charles: you'll inscribe her yet upon your catalogue, you old Don Juan: but you won't have any further need of Chaumontel's affair; I'm no longer jealous, you've got a passport. Do you like that better than being adored? Monster, observe how considerate I am."

So soon as her husband has gone, Caroline, who had not omitted, the previous evening, to write to Ferdinand to come to breakfast with her, equips herself in a costume which, in that charming eighteenth century so calumniated by republicans, humanitarians and idiots, women of quality called their fighting-dress.

Caroline has taken care of everything. Love is the first house servant in the world, so the table is set with positively diabolic coquetry.

There is the white damask cloth, the little blue service, the silver gilt urn, the chiseled milk pitcher, and flowers all round!

If it is winter, she has got some grapes, and has rummaged the cellar for the very best old wine. The rolls are from the most famous baker's. The succulent dishes, the *pate de foie gras*, the whole of this elegant entertainment, would have made the author of the Glutton's Almanac neigh with impatience: it would make a note-shaver smile, and tell a professor of the old University what the matter in hand is.

Everything is prepared. Caroline has been ready since the night before: she contemplates her work. Justine sighs and arranges the furniture. Caroline picks off the yellow leaves of the plants in the windows. A woman, in these cases, disguises what we may call the prancings of the heart, by those meaningless occupations in which the fingers have all the grip of pincers, when the pink nails burn, and when this unspoken exclamation rasps the throat: "He hasn't come yet!"

What a blow is this announcement by Justine: "Madame, here's a letter!"

A letter in place of Ferdinand! How does she ever open it? What ages of life slip by as she unfolds it! Women know this by experience! As to men, when they are in such maddening passes, they murder their shirt-frills.

"Justine, Monsieur Ferdinand is ill!" exclaims Caroline. "Send for a carriage."

As Justine goes down stairs, Adolphe comes up.

"My poor mistress!" observes Justine. "I guess she won't want the carriage now."

"Oh my! Where have you come from?" cries Caroline, on seeing Adolphe standing in ecstasy before her voluptuous breakfast.

Adolphe, whose wife long since gave up treating *him* to such charming banquets, does not answer. But he guesses what it all means, as he sees the cloth inscribed with the delightful ideas which Madame de Fischtaminel or the syndic of Chaumontel's affair have often inscribed for him upon tables quite as elegant.

"Whom are you expecting?" he asks in his turn.

"Who could it be, except Ferdinand?" replies Caroline.

"And is he keeping you waiting?"

"He is sick, poor fellow."

A quizzical idea enters Adolphe's head, and he replies, winking with one eye only: "I have just seen him."

"Where?"

"In front of the Cafe de Paris, with some friends."

"But why have you come back?" says Caroline, trying to conceal her murderous fury.

"Madame Foullepointe, who was tired of Charles, you said, has been with him at Ville d'Avray since yesterday."

Adolphe sits down, saying: "This has happened very appropriately, for I'm as hungry as two bears."

Caroline sits down, too, and looks at Adolphe stealthily: she weeps internally: but she very soon asks, in a tone of voice that she manages to render indifferent, "Who was Ferdinand with?"

"With some fellows who lead him into bad company. The young man is getting spoiled: he goes to Madame Schontz's. You ought to write to your uncle. It was probably some breakfast or other, the result of a bet made at M'lle Malaga's." He looks slyly at Caroline, who drops her eyes to conceal her tears. "How beautiful you have made yourself this morning," Adolphe resumes. "Ah, you are a fair match for your breakfast. I don't think Ferdinand will make as good a meal as I shall," etc., etc.

Adolphe manages the joke so cleverly that he inspires his wife with the idea of punishing Ferdinand. Adolphe, who claims to be as hungry as two bears, causes Caroline to forget that a carriage waits for her at the door.

The female that tends the gate at the house Ferdinand lives in, arrives at about two o'clock, while Adolphe is asleep on a sofa. That Iris of bachelors comes to say to Caroline that Monsieur Ferdinand is very much in need of some one.

"He's drunk, I suppose," says Caroline in a rage.

"He fought a duel this morning, madame."

Caroline swoons, gets up and rushes to Ferdinand, wishing Adolphe at the bottom of the sea.

When women are the victims of these little inventions, which are quite as adroit as their own, they are sure to exclaim, "What abominable monsters men are!"

ULTIMA RATIO.

We have come to our last observation. Doubtless this work is beginning to tire you quite as much as its subject does, if you are married.

This work, which, according to the author, is to the *Physiology of Marriage* what Fact is to Theory, or History to Philosophy, has its logic, as life, viewed as a whole, has its logic, also.

This logic—fatal, terrible—is as follows. At the close of the first part of the book—a book filled with serious pleasantry—Adolphe has reached, as you must have noticed, a point of complete indifference in matrimonial matters.

He has read novels in which the writers advise troublesome husbands to embark for the other world, or to live in peace with the fathers of their children, to pet and adore them: for if literature is the reflection of manners, we must admit that our manners recognize the defects pointed out by the *Physiology of Marriage* in this fundamental institution. More than one great genius has dealt this social basis terrible blows, without shaking it.

Adolphe has especially read his wife too closely, and disguises his indifference by this profound word: indulgence. He is indulgent with Caroline, he sees in her nothing but the mother of his children, a good companion, a sure friend, a brother.

When the petty troubles of the wife cease, Caroline, who is more clever than her husband, has come to profit by this advantageous indulgence: but she does not give her dear Adolphe up. It is woman's nature never to yield any of her rights. DIEU ET MON DROIT—CONJUGAL! is, as is well known, the motto of England, and is especially so to-day.

Women have such a love of domination that we will relate an anecdote, not ten years old, in point. It is a very young anecdote.

One of the grand dignitaries of the Chamber of Peers had a Caroline, as lax as Carolines usually are. The name is an auspicious one for women. This dignitary, extremely old at the time, was on one side of the fireplace, and Caroline on the other. Caroline was hard upon the lustrum when women no longer tell their age. A friend came in to inform them of the marriage of a general who had lately been intimate in their house.

Caroline at once had a fit of despair, with genuine tears; she screamed and made the grand dignitary's head ache to such a degree, that he tried to console her. In the midst of his condolences, the count forgot himself so far as to say — "What can you expect, my dear, he really could not marry you!"

And this was one of the highest functionaries of the state, but a friend of Louis XVIII, and necessarily a little bit Pompadour.

The whole difference, then, between the situation of Adolphe and that of Caroline, consists in this: though he no longer cares about her, she retains the right to care about him.

Now, let us listen to "What *they* say," the theme of the concluding chapter of this work.

COMMENTARY.

IN WHICH IS EXPLAINED LA FELICITA OF FINALES.

Who has not heard an Italian opera in the course of his life? You must then have noticed the musical abuse of the word *felicita*, so lavishly used by the librettist and the chorus at the moment when everybody is deserting his box or leaving the house.

Frightful image of life. We quit it just when we hear *la felicita*.

Have you reflected upon the profound truth conveyed by this finale, at the instant when the composer delivers his last note and the author his last line, when the orchestra gives the last pull at the fiddle-bow and the last puff at the bassoon, when the principal singers say "Let's go to supper!" and the chorus people exclaim "How lucky, it doesn't rain!" Well, in every condition in life, as in an Italian opera, there comes a time when the joke is over, when the trick is done, when people must make up their minds to one thing or the other, when everybody is singing his own *felicita* for himself. After having gone through with all the duos, the solos, the stretti, the codas, the concerted pieces, the duettos, the nocturnes, the phases which these few scenes, chosen from the ocean of married life, exhibit you, and which are themes whose variations have doubtless been divined by persons with brains as well as by the shallow — for so far as suffering is concerned, we are all equal — the greater part of Parisian households reach, without a given time, the following final chorus:

THE WIFE, *to a young woman in the conjugal Indian Summer*. My dear, I am the happiest woman in the world. Adolphe is the model of husbands, kind, obliging, not a bit of a tease. Isn't he, Ferdinand?

Caroline addresses Adolphe's cousin, a young man with a nice cravat, glistening hair and patent leather boots: his coat is cut in the most elegant fashion: he has a crush hat, kid gloves, something very choice in the way of a waistcoat, the very best style of moustaches, whiskers, and a goatee a la Mazarin; he is also endowed with a profound, mute, attentive admiration of Caroline.

FERDINAND. Adolphe is happy to have a wife like you! What does he want? Nothing.

THE WIFE. In the beginning, we were always vexing each other: but now we get along marvelously. Adolphe no longer does anything but what he likes, he never puts himself out: I never ask him where he is going nor what he has seen. Indulgence, my dear, is the great secret of happiness. You, doubtless, are still in the period of petty troubles, causeless jealousies, cross-purposes, and all sorts of little botherations. What is the good of all this? We women have but a short life, at the best. How much? Ten good years! Why should we fill them with vexation? I was like you. But, one fine morning, I made the acquaintance of Madame de Fischtaminel, a charming woman, who taught me how to make a husband happy. Since then, Adolphe has changed radically; he has become perfectly delightful. He is the first to say to me, with anxiety, with alarm, even, when I am going to the theatre, and he and I are still alone at seven o'clock: "Ferdinand is coming for you, isn't he?" Doesn't he, Ferdinand?

FERDINAND. We are the best cousins in the world.

THE INDIAN SUMMER WIFE, *very much affected.* Shall I ever come to that?

THE HUSBAND, *on the Italian Boulevard.* My dear boy [he has button-holed Monsieur de Fischtaminel], you still believe that marriage is based upon passion. Let me tell you that the best way, in conjugal life, is to have a plenary indulgence, one for the other, on condition that appearances be preserved. I am the happiest husband in the world. Caroline is a devoted friend, she would sacrifice everything for me, even my cousin Ferdinand, if it were necessary: oh, you may laugh, but she is ready to do anything. You entangle yourself in your laughable ideas of dignity, honor, virtue, social order. We can't have our life over again, so we must cram it full of pleasure. Not the smallest bitter word has been exchanged between Caroline and me for two years past. I have, in Caroline, a friend to whom I can tell everything, and who would be amply able to console me in a great emergency. There is not the slightest deceit between us, and we know perfectly well what the state of things is. We have thus changed our duties into pleasures. We are often happier, thus, than in that insipid season called the honey-moon. She says to me, sometimes, "I'm out of humor, go away." The storm then falls upon my cousin. Caroline never puts on her airs of a victim, now, but speaks in the kindest manner of me to the whole world. In short, she is happy in my pleasures. And as she is a scrupulously honest woman, she is conscientious to the last degree in her use of our fortune. My house is well kept. My wife leaves me the right to dispose of my reserve without the slightest control on her part. That's the way of it. We have oiled our wheels and cogs, while you, my dear Fischtaminel, have put gravel in yours.

CHORUS, *in a parlor during a ball.* Madame Caroline is a charming woman.

A WOMAN IN A TURBAN. Yes, she is very proper, very dignified.

A WOMAN WHO HAS SEVEN CHILDREN. Ah! she learned early how to manage her husband.

ONE OF FERDINAND'S FRIENDS. But she loves her husband exceedingly. Besides, Adolphe is a man of great distinction and experience.

ONE OF MADAME DE FISCHTAMINEL'S FRIENDS. He adores his wife. There's no fuss at their house, everybody is at home there.

MONSIEUR FOULLEPOINTE. Yes, it's a very agreeable house.

A WOMAN ABOUT WHOM THERE IS A GOOD DEAL OF SCANDAL. Caroline is kind and obliging, and never talks scandal of anybody.

A YOUNG LADY, *returning to her place after a dance.* Don't you remember how tiresome she was when she visited the Deschars?

MADAME DE FISCHTAMINEL. Oh! She and her husband were two bundles of briars—continually quarreling. [She goes away.]

AN ARTIST. I hear that the individual known as Deschars is getting dissipated: he goes round town—

A WOMAN, *alarmed at the turn the conversation is taking, as her daughter can hear.* Madame de Fischtaminel is charming, this evening.

A WOMAN OF FORTY, *without employment.* Monsieur Adolphe appears to be as happy as his wife.

A YOUNG LADY. Oh! what a sweet man Monsieur Ferdinand is! [Her mother reproves her by a sharp nudge with her foot.] What's the matter, mamma?

HER MOTHER, *looking at her fixedly*. A young woman should not speak so, my dear, of any one but her betrothed, and Monsieur Ferdinand is not a marrying man.

A LADY DRESSED RATHER LOW IN THE NECK, *to another lady dressed equally low, in a whisper*. The fact is, my dear, the moral of all this is that there are no happy couples but couples of four.

A FRIEND, *whom the author was so imprudent as to consult*. Those last words are false.

THE AUTHOR. Do you think so?

THE FRIEND, *who has just been married*. You all of you use your ink in depreciating social life, on the pretext of enlightening us! Why, there are couples a hundred, a thousand times happier than your boasted couples of four.

THE AUTHOR. Well, shall I deceive the marrying class of the population, and scratch the passage out?

THE FRIEND. No, it will be taken merely as the point of a song in a vaudeville.

THE AUTHOR. Yes, a method of passing truths off upon society.

THE FRIEND, *who sticks to his opinion*. Such truths as are destined to be passed off upon it.

THE AUTHOR, *who wants to have the last word*. Who and what is there that does not pass off, or become passe? When your wife is twenty years older, we will resume this conversation.

THE FRIEND. You revenge yourself cruelly for your inability to write the history of happy homes.

THE END